MW01128153

SHIFTER'S SHADOW

LEGION OF ANGELS: BOOK 5

ELLA SUMMERS

SHIFTER'S SHADOW

Legion of Angels: Book 5

www.ellasummers.com/shifters-shadow

ISBN 978-1-5486-5453-5

Dragon Born Alexandria

Magic Edge

Blood Magic

Magic Kingdom

Dragon Born Awakening

Fairy Magic

And more books coming soon…

CHAPTERS

THE NEW ANGEL

*E*veryone had gathered in the center of the canteen, where the tables had been cleared away to make room for a platform. High above this spot, the points of the gigantic star in the glass ceiling slid apart. Warm, golden light spilled inside. A black and blond shape shot down, landing on the platform in a crouch. Slowly, his dark wings spread open, black with bright brilliant blue accents.

My heart sank when I realized it wasn't Nero at all. The angel rose from the ground. Shock trailed surprise when I saw his face. It was Harker, the soldier who had been my friend, the soldier who had betrayed me. Harker was an angel now.

"Legion soldiers of New York," he said. "By order of the First Angel, I am taking command of this facility."

His words hung in the room for a few seconds, like a music note in an opera hall. Every person in the canteen was staring at him, but no one spoke. The room was as quiet as a graveyard.

Harker's gaze panned across his captive audience, his blue eyes sparkling with magic. Angel magic. They burned like an electric storm—sizzling, popping, building up for an explosion. His dark wings, the ink-dipped tips as glossy as obsidian, spread wider. They seemed to drink in all the light in the room.

Standing there on that platform, his wings extended to the heavens, he looked larger than life.

He met my eyes, the silence stretching into eternity. And when he finally spoke again, he seemed to be speaking to me directly.

"The demons are on the move," he said, his voice filling the empty silence. "They have been striking out from the shadows for years, but recently, they've grown bolder. It is only a matter of time before they attack us outright. The First Angel has charged me with preparing you for the great battle to come. We will need more soldiers, stronger soldiers. We will need angels."

His eyes bored into me like a diamond drill. Electric sparks sizzled across his blue irises, his magic so intense that my eyes watered. Still, I didn't look away. This was a game.

"Things here will be different than they were under Colonel Fireswift's warm embrace," Harker said.

A few people laughed.

"The massacres will end," Harker continued, his eyes panning across the crowd. "A promotion ceremony is not a culling. Only those soldiers who are ready to drink the gods' next gift will participate. Your lives are too precious to us to waste."

The soldiers around me noticeably relaxed. Colonel Fireswift was a sadistic man who would sacrifice a hundred soldiers to gain the Legion a single angel. No one missed him.

Harker turned, and the sunlight streaming through the windows twinkled off the silver symbol pinned onto his black leather uniform. The small metal emblem depicted a pair of wings. It was the mark of a Legion soldier of the eighth level, of his distinguished rank as an angel. And below the pin, stitched in a clear, no-nonsense font were the words 'Lt. Colonel Sunstorm'. So that was his new name.

When a Legion soldier became an angel, he or she was bestowed with a new surname—an angelic surname—to celebrate their elevated status. Angels passed on that name to any children they sired. Legion brats, a nickname for the offspring of an angel, inherited more advantages than just a high magical potential. Their name opened doors for them, showing them with privileges the rest of us could only dream of.

Harker's voice filled the room once more. "I won't lie to you. I won't *ever* lie to you." He met my eyes again. "The easy days are behind us. A new era dawns. Now, more than ever, you need to grow your magic, to make yourself strong for the days to come."

Be strong for the days to come. That was the Legion of Angels in a nutshell. We had to always train, always grow our magic, for that day the demons returned to wage war on the Earth.

"We will recruit new soldiers, more than ever before," said Harker. His words wove a spell around the crowd, drawing them in. Mesmerizing them. "You will *all* need to train and level up your magic. And when the demons come, we will be ready for them."

His feathers rustled lightly, as though caught in a breeze. But that was no natural breeze cutting through the room. It was magic—a soft, silky magic that slid against my senses, embracing me, inviting me to let go and allow the angel to save me from the horrors of this world. I need only follow his lead. Everything would be just fine.

The smirk on his face snapped me out of the trance. He had brought the whole room under the spell of his siren's song. His magic had grown enormously since becoming an angel, and he wasn't shy about showing it. He was trying to exert some influence over me, trying to make me have warm feelings for him. He'd always wanted to be an angel, so it came as no surprise to me that he was diving right into the angel games.

Harker lifted his hands. A wave of magic—that same soft, silky magic—rippled across the room. Everyone around me knelt at once, swept up by the power of his compulsion.

Everyone except for me.

I'd always had a natural resistance to the sirens' songs. Or angels' songs, for that matter. Shortly after joining the Legion, Nero had tried the same trick on me that Harker was using now. It hadn't worked then either. I stood tall and met Harker's eyes, allowing a smile to curl my lips.

He stepped off the platform, moving through the crowd of kneeling soldiers like a giant through a field of tiny tulips. The smile never left his face, even as he stopped in front of me.

"You're supposed to kneel, Pandora," he said casually, his voice dipped low.

I lifted my brows at the sound of my nickname. It was the nickname Nero had given me. Harker spoke the name just like Nero—with that same hard edge. Hard but not cruel.

But Harker hadn't been an angel nearly as long as Nero had. There were cracks in his armor. I could see the strain in his face as he tried to compel me to kneel—and the frustration in his eyes when I did not go down easily.

"You're still not kneeling," he told me.

I smiled.

"This is how things are done at the Legion." Despite himself, he actually looked amused. Even as he stood there in his big, black uniform with his big, black wings. Even as he chastised me for my lack of protocol and respect. He set his hands on my shoulders. His touch was firm, but he was forcing me down. "You're drawing attention to yourself."

I looked around. He spoke the truth. Some of the other soldiers were staring at me in shock.

"It isn't common to resist an angel's compulsion." Harker's tone was borderline casual. "They're going to start asking what you really are."

"And what am I?" I asked, my defiance somewhat diminished by my burning desire to know.

He shook his head. "I don't know, but I'm sure it will come out eventually. Unique magic has a habit of not staying buried."

I opened my mouth to say something, but what could I say? I didn't know what I was, nor did I know where I'd come from.

"Who me?" I said with perfect innocence, a smile on my face. "I'm just a regular girl from the Frontier of civilization."

"We both know that's not true, Leda."

I kept smiling. Even if I had known something, I wouldn't have told him. Sure, we'd recently worked together to save Storm Castle, but I was living under no delusions that Harker was trustworthy. He was too ambitious to gain magic, to level up in the Legion. And he was too loyal to the mystery god he served. That loyalty had obviously paid off. It must be the reason he'd been made into an angel.

The bigger question was why the First Angel had agreed to make Harker an angel. She didn't trust him. She wouldn't have kept him locked up for months if she did. Maybe she hadn't had a choice. If a god commanded her to make someone an angel, could she say no? Nyx was a fighter, but sometimes you had to cut the crap and go with the flow. I looked at the growing number of eyes on me. Perhaps, now was one of those times.

I was about to kneel, anything to blend in, to not draw attention to myself, when I felt another ripple of magic slide across me like a warm, balmy breeze. I turned to find Nero walking across the room.

His black leather uniform shifted deliciously against his muscular body as he moved forward in hard, powerful strides. Each step was like a pulsing punch of energy. His wings—a tapestry of black, blue, and green feathers—were extended high and wide in a show of strength. He looked huge, even bigger than Harker. Like a predator on the prowl.

Nero stopped beside me, nearly shoulder-to-shoulder. He took my hand.

"The mate of an angel does not kneel before another angel," he said, his voice as hard as granite, his eyes as unforgiving as green diamonds. "You and I are one. For you to kneel would be for *me* to kneel."

In other words, it would make Nero look weak. He was a soldier of the ninth level. He did not kneel before other angels, least of all lower-level angels.

"I didn't know," I told Nero.

The truth was I didn't know a lot of things, especially when it came to the ways of angels. That's what I got for jumping in head first, for deciding to be Nero's mate. But, even now, I didn't regret it a bit. I loved Nero. I could put up with the games of angels if it meant we were together.

One of Nero's wings brushed against my back. It was a sign of support, his way of telling me that even when he sounded hard and unforgiving, he wasn't mad at me. He had my back.

"But I'm sure you were about to tell her that," he said to Harker.

The other angel smiled. "Of course."

Nero's expression was masked, but that calm icy facade didn't fool me. Hints of emotion seeped through our bond—surprise and worry and some other emotions brewing deep beneath the surface. Harker's appearance, his promotion, had thrown Nero for a loop. He hadn't known Harker was coming to be the new head of the Legion's New York office.

But then what was Nero's news? Why had Nyx sent him here?

The two angels continued to stare at each other in silence, the tension growing between them like a thick fog bubbling up from a witch's cauldron. They looked ready to fight. That was just what we did *not* need right now.

I squeezed Nero's hand.

That seemed to snap him out of it. "Come with me," he said to me.

Then he turned his back on Harker and headed toward the exit, golden and silver magic sizzling across his wings like a fireworks show. To say Nero was agitated would have been an enormous understatement. I didn't have to be a telepath to know what was going through his head right now. As far as Nero was concerned, the only thing worse than Harker's promotion and appointment to the New York office was that he hadn't known about it.

I walked beside Nero, the hard soles of our boots echoing through the silence. I glanced past the faces in the crowd. Some people smiled at me, some frowned. The Legion of Angels as a whole fell into two distinct camps: people who really liked me, and people who couldn't stand me. The representation in this room was no different.

"Leda," Nero said as soon as we were in the hallway, the

doors closed behind us. "I have something important to tell you."

"I take it this has to do with the reason you are here?"

"Yes."

"I really thought you were back here permanently, that you were in charge of the New York office again. I thought *that* was your news."

"No." The word was equal parts regret and resignation. "Nyx's concerns about us haven't changed."

The First Angel was under the impression that I was a bad influence on Nero. She wasn't wrong. I got him mixed up in all kinds of shenanigans.

"Then why are you here?" I asked him.

"The wait is over. Nyx has given me my next assignment." He paused. He sure did know how to keep me on my toes.

"Well? What is it? Bloodthirsty vampires? Dark angels trying to take over the world?"

Nero snorted. "Vampires are always bloodthirsty. And dark angels are always trying to take over the world." His face grew serious. "It's time for my promotion test, the Gods' Trials. That is the task Nyx has given me. And you, if you still wish to be my second."

"Of course I do. Without me, you'll just get into trouble."

"I find that an unusual statement coming from you."

I grinned. He didn't call me Pandora for nothing.

"When does it happen?" I asked.

"Now. We leave immediately. We have an appointment to keep with the God of War."

2

THE BATTLE MAIDEN OF NEW YORK

I gazed out the window of the airship, down at the scorched sands of the Western Wilderness. The blanket of desert stretched as far as my supernatural eyes could see, punctuated only by the occasional cactus or a low plateau of red-orange stones. The only animals that lived out here were insects and the roaming herds of monsters.

One of those herds had just come around a plateau. They looked like a cross between wild horses and bison. The sun's unrelenting rays shone hard against their long, crimson-tipped horns, giving them a glossy glow—like the beasts had painted their horns with the blood of anyone unfortunate enough to be wandering these forsaken lands. Their equally-crimson hooves trampled across the cracked ground, kicking up a sandstorm of dust that followed in the herd's wake.

"No time for daydreaming, Pandora," Nero said behind me.

I turned away from the window and faced him, hastily rebinding my bloody hands. Nero and I had spent the past four hours—basically, every moment since we'd boarded the airship in New York—training in this onboard gym. The

9

God of War hadn't yet graced us with his presence, so we'd filled the time by kicking ass. Actually, the ass-kicking had been decidedly one-sided, as training often was with Nero. We'd started with endurance training, then moved on to pain resistance. I looked down at my bloody hands. I hated pain resistance training.

Of course, Nero heard my thoughts. "To survive the Gods' Trials, we will need both our mental strength and will," he said aloud. "We can't rely on our magic. The trials will strip us of our powers one-by-one until we have no magic left."

And that's what made the level ten promotion different from every one that had come before. We trained for each new level by practicing that power—or, more often, our resistance to that power—to prime our magic for the Nectar. But this was a different kind of test. For this test, the test for the highest angel level, Nero wasn't priming a power. He would be stripped of his magic and then thrown into some unknown crisis to see how he dealt with it.

"What kind of magic do angels of the tenth level gain?" I asked him.

Every other level in the Legion of Angels was defined by an ability. Each level was named for that ability. Vampire's Kiss gave Legion initiates the powers of strength, speed, and stamina; it also allowed them to heal quickly when drinking the blood of others. Witch's Cauldron gave them the powers of potion brewing. Siren's Song, Dragon's Storm, Shifter's Shadow…and so on, all the way up to level ten, the final level. But level ten had no name.

"Level ten has no name because there is no single ability tied to it," Nero explained. "The Nectar I will drink is pure Nectar. In addition to strengthening my previous powers, I will gain a new power. Or perhaps more than one. You never know before you drink."

When I'd first joined the Legion, I'd drunk a heavily diluted Nectar. It had killed half of us, but those who survived grew stronger. That tiny hint of Nectar primed our magic. When we'd sipped a stronger Nectar the next time, more of us survived, and those that did gained the gods' first gift of magic. With each new level, the Nectar was less diluted. Level ten was pure Nectar, the food of the gods. It made angels as close to the gods as any human could be. And so it made sense that every soldier of the tenth level—every archangel— had their own unique powers, just like the gods did.

"We are done with my training for now," Nero said.

He unwrapped his own bloody hands. He hadn't healed himself either. He'd told me that the trials wouldn't be decided by magic but by tenacity. That was just a fancy word for stubbornness.

"It's your turn," he told me, walking toward the door.

Yeah, that wasn't foreboding at all.

"If there's a monster behind that door, I'm going to let it eat you," I promised as I tried to salvage what was left of my bloody bandages.

The door opened, and Alec Morrows stepped into the gym. He gave me a long, assessing look, then declared, "Whoa, Leda. You look like shit."

I shot him a saccharine smile. "Thanks. That makes me feel much better."

He swept into a bow. "Glad to be of service."

His dramatics cleared the doorway, allowing Ivy and Drake to squeeze past his juggernaut body. Claudia strode in after them, the battle maiden of New York. She had the kind of voluptuous curves that turned heads wherever she went, but she wasn't soft. She was stronger than Alec and Drake, the New York Legion office's go-to muscle men, and she could shoot the eyelashes off a dragonfly from hundred feet away. Or so the urban legend said. I wasn't sure dragonflies even had eyelashes.

"Hey, Leda," she greeted me.

Alec winked at her.

"Morrows, direct your eyes higher, or you'll be staring at my fist."

"Oh, I wasn't looking at your assets. Honest." He was almost convincing. Almost. I knew Alec too well to be fooled. "I was just admiring your new pin, Lieutenant Vance."

Sure enough, 'Lt. Vance' was stitched into her jacket. That must have happened when I was away at Storm Castle, during one of Colonel Fireswift's mass level-up-or-die promotions. At least Harker was putting an end to those.

"Congratulations," I told Claudia.

Claudia touched the metal pin on her jacket, the symbol of her magic rank. It was the shape of a wolf paw, the universal symbol for shifting magic. Werewolves weren't the only type of shifters, but they were the most famous. Or perhaps *infamous* was the better word.

Claudia smiled at me. "It's your turn now."

"Yes," Nero agreed, as his psychic gust slammed the door shut. "It is your turn, Leda." He looked at Ivy, Drake, Claudia, and Alec. "Leda is training for the fifth level, the power of Shifter's Shadow, and she needs your help. Due to my own trials and her role in them, time is tight. I've summoned you here because Leda considers you friends."

Alec gaped at me. "Even me?"

"Na, you're just here because you hit hard," I told him.

Alec chuckled.

Nero looked at me. "Shifting has mental and physical components. You can actually change your appearance—what is called a physical shift. Or you can create an illusion —a mental shift, often referred to as glamour."

I nodded.

"Werewolves and other shifters perform physical shifts," he continued. "A physical shift is more complete; others cannot see through it. Soldiers of the Legion usually opt for a mental shift because it requires substantially less magic. A physical shift is a constant drain on your magic. It takes so much out of you that you cannot use any other powers at the same time. That works for shifters, whose magic is their strength and their claws. But as a Legion soldier, you use many powers in parallel. For that reason, we tend to prefer a mental shift over a physical one."

Nero motioned Claudia forward. "We are going to train your shifting magic the same way you trained your elemental magic: by building up your resistance."

"You want me to resist shifting my shape?" I asked, confused.

"No, I want you to resist the mental magic woven by someone who is casting it," he explained. "Lieutenant Vance is going to use her shifting magic, and you have to see through the spell. Just remember: the higher the level of the person casting a spell, the harder it is to see through the illusion."

At a nod from Nero, Claudia waved her hand in front of Ivy, Drake, and Alec. Magic rippled across their bodies, snapping like a rubber band. And then there were four Claudias in front of me.

I blinked. "Amazing. You all look just like her."

One of the Claudias looked down at her chest and smirked. "We really do." That was definitely Alec.

"Morrows, what did I say about you ogling my breasts?" the real Claudia warned him.

Alec's smirk persisted. "They are *my* breasts now."

Nero gave them a hard stare. They stopped bickering and stood still, like perfect soldiers.

Then he looked at me. "Close your eyes."

I closed them. I could hear my friends shuffling positions.

"Ok, Leda," Nero said.

When I opened my eyes again, the four Claudias were circling around me. I couldn't for the life of me figure out who was who. They looked like quadruplets.

"Your task is to tag the real Lieutenant Vance," Nero told me.

I squinted at them, trying to pick out any differences, even minor ones. But they not only looked the same—they moved the same. Claudia had done a good job on them, masking their individuality with her magic. They all looked like her, talked like her, moved like her. Even the two big guys. I just kept watching them, hoping for inspiration to hit me.

One of the Claudias hit me first. I recovered my balance and moved around her so that all four of them were in front of me. I wasn't going to let them sneak up on me again.

"Come on, Pandora," Nero called out. His words were both an encouragement that I could do this *and* a reminder to get a move on.

Yes, come on, Leda, I told myself.

Back in the Lost City, I'd been able to see through Nero's shifting magic, and he was a lot more powerful than Claudia. I could do this. Of course, at the time, I'd just exchanged a few pints of blood with Nero, so my magic and blood were completely in tune with his. And I'd seen through Damiel's shift because he was Nero's father, and the two of them shared blood.

I couldn't cheat this time. I hadn't exchanged blood or slept with any one of the four Claudias.

"Time's up, Pandora." Nero waved the Claudia army forward.

They all rushed me in a storm of punches and kicks. I evaded most of their attacks. I endured the others. After the agony of my pain resistance training with Nero, I hardly felt the blows. But fighting four opponents at once kept me too busy to concentrate on seeing through the shift.

"What do you think you're doing, Nero?" I demanded. If I could have spared him a scowl, I would have.

"Helping."

One of the Claudias hit me in the head. I felt *that*. It must have been Drake or Alec. They hit hard. But, then again, so did the real Claudia. This was so frustrating!

"You call this helping?!"

"Yes," Nero replied calmly.

Another fist slammed against my head. I slipped aside to avoid the follow-up. It was then—in that moment I moved aside—that I realized something. Nero was right. It was easy to maintain an illusion when they were just talking or walking. But the illusion cracked under the complexity of a fight. Every one of them had a different style, different moves. This was where the cracks in Claudia's spell showed. She couldn't maintain such a complex illusion. I could see them now.

Alec and Drake charged at me from two sides. I darted past them, zigzagged around Ivy, then ran straight for Claudia.

"You're it," I said and tagged her on the shoulder.

Claudia laughed, and the last remnants of her spell fizzled out.

"Hey, I'm pretty good at this," I said, throwing Nero a triumphant smirk

"Oh, Pandora," he replied. "That was merely the warm-up. We're just getting started."

***

AFTER THAT 'WARM-UP', CLAUDIA AND HER MAGIC clones armed themselves with lightning whips. I, on the other hand, was armed with nothing but my charming smile. I didn't bother complaining about the unfairness of the fight. I'd learned long ago that Nero didn't believe in fairness when it came to training Legion soldiers. He said fairness—like luck and coffee—was a crutch you shouldn't depend on.

The bite of the lightning whips took me down faster than my opponents' fists could. I must have passed out a good dozen times on that floor before I managed to see the truth behind Claudia's shifting spell.

Nero rewarded my achievement by arming my opponents with guns that shot magic stun pellets. That allowed them to knock me on my ass even faster.

With each phase of the training session, I had less time to see through the illusions, less time to find the real Claudia. On the bright side, I got to spend a lot of quality time on the floor.

"You won't improve by napping during training, Pandora," Nero chided me as I tried—and failed—to push off the ground.

My sides hurt. My head hurt. Every inch of my body, inside and out, hurt.

"Nero Windstriker, you are a sick, sadistic *miscreant*."

I picked the word I thought would annoy him the most. Rules and procedures were the bread and butter of his life.

Calling him a lawbreaker should have solicited at least a frown.

The angel's mouth didn't even twitch. "Less talking, more standing."

I clenched my jaw hard and peeled my aching body off the floor. I staggered to my feet, holding my hand to my bruised side. My opponents stared in morbid fascination at the inky patterns of black and blue quickly spreading across my skin. I looked like a peach that had been dropped on the floor—and then put through the garbage disposal for good measure.

"Why are you four just standing there?" Nero demanded. "Shoot her."

Glowing pellets burst out of their guns like shooting stars. Desperate, I drew on my dark elemental magic, hurling a stream of fire at the incoming pellets. They disintegrated.

"Cool," I muttered out of my bruised lips.

A few minutes ago, I'd tried the same spell with light magic, and the pellets had gone right through like the fire wasn't even there. Some people considered light magic good and dark magic evil, but they were really just two sides of the same magic coin. Dark tore into light magic and light tore into dark. That's why my dark magic fire had worked where my light-based fire had failed. The guns shot light-magic pellets, resistant to light magic, weak against dark.

My opponents tried again. This time, I put more power behind the fire. The resulting reaction of pellets and dark fire created an invisible magical explosion that rippled across the gym, tearing through Claudia's spell. The illusion shattered, revealing my opponents' true faces.

"Cool," I said again.

Ivy was standing the closest to me. I slammed my fist into her arm, disarming her. I caught her gun before it fell and used it to shoot Claudia in the leg. She growled in pain, clutching a blossoming bruise.

"Got you," I told her.

The slow, steady crack of clapping hands echoed off the walls. I spun toward the door. A man stood there, dressed in a suit of fitted battle leather as black as his hair. A pair of wings folded out from his back, wings unlike any I had ever seen. The feathers sparkled like diamonds in the moonlight.

"Lord Ronan," Nero said.

Ronan was the God of War and Lord of the Legion of Angels, the gods' army on Earth.

3

THE GOD OF WAR

*M*y friends knelt before Ronan, their heads bowed low. Claudia lowered with difficulty thanks to the swelling bruise in her leg.

I looked at Nero. Were we supposed to kneel before the gods? I didn't want to make the same mistake I'd almost made with Harker. Dating an angel really should have come with a guidebook. The book that Nero had given me, the illustrated guide on the ways of angels, didn't cover the finer points of etiquette.

Nero took my hand. *Yes,* he said in my mind. *Angels and their mates kneel before the gods.*

Of course they did. Nero and I had knelt before Nyx, and she was only a demigod.

I mimicked Nero's slow, graceful drop into his knees. I'd never seen anyone genuflect with such elegance and dignity. He kept his gaze lifted toward the god in our midst. Ronan walked around my friends, not sparing them a second glance —or a first one, for that matter. He stopped in front of me and Nero.

"Nero Windstriker, you and your mate may rise."

As we rose from the ground, I tried not to stare too hard at Ronan. This was Nyx's boss, Lord of the Legion of Angels. A god stood in front of me, in the flesh. He was the only god I'd ever seen. Besides the heavenly glow of his skin—and the fact that he was taller than anyone I'd ever seen in my life—he didn't look much different than the rest of us. Nyx was romantically involved with one of the gods. Was Ronan her godly lover?

He gave me a hard, penetrating look, as though he could see right through me.

Control your thoughts, Leda, Nero chided me silently.

Sorry.

The gods were telepathic. I had to refrain from internal commentary in their presence.

"My apologies, Lord Ronan. She is new to our ways. I take full responsibility for any offense she has caused," Nero said smoothly.

He'd also apologized to Nyx about me during my first meeting with her. I really needed to get my thoughts under control.

"The time has come, Nero," Ronan said.

His voice was so normal. I'd always imagined a god's voice would rumble more. Maybe shake the walls a little.

"I can do that too," he told me.

Crap. I was thinking too loudly again.

Ronan looked at my friends. "Leave us." When he spoke this time, his voice boomed like thunder, shaking the floors and walls of the airship.

They jumped to their feet and bolted out of the room. They'd never moved that fast during training. They hadn't even moved that fast when beasts and baddies were chasing them on the battlefield.

When Nero and I were alone with Ronan, the Lord of

the Legion glanced down at our hands. "You're injured." He waved his hand in front of us.

A warm, tingly feeling permeated my body, and my wounds sealed before my eyes. I wiggled my fingers. Even my broken pinky finger was back to normal.

"If you are going to fail, let it be said that you failed fairly," declared Ronan.

I blinked at him and shrugged with all my will to keep my mind blank.

Ronan turned and began to walk toward the stairs. "Come with me."

Nero took my hand, and we followed Ronan as he ascended the stairs up to the observation deck. Up top, there weren't any walls or windows. It was open space. The warm wind blew in my face, rustling my hair all around me.

"Your soldiers must return to New York now, Colonel Windstriker," Ronan said. "It is just you. And your companion." He looked me over closely. I had the distinct impression that he was dissecting me with his eyes. "Are you sure you want her to be your second? She is so…young. So frail."

"Yes." Nero didn't even hesitate, and I loved him for it. "She's stronger than she looks." He squeezed my hand.

"So Nyx says," replied Ronan. "Very well. Then let us waste no time. What do you know of the City of Ashes?"

"It is a city that sits at the western edge of the Western Wilderness," said Nero. "It once sat on the right side of civilization. But a few years after the walls went up to separate humanity from the monsters, the Magitech barrier protecting the City of Ashes failed, and the city fell. The wild lands swallowed it up, and it has been lost to us ever since."

"The gods have decided it is time humanity reclaimed the city," Ronan told us. "The magic barrier suffered from a magic failure, but the structure of the wall is still mainly intact. Your mission is to journey into the City of Ashes and repair the Magitech barrier. Once it's back up, a magic wave will sweep through the city and every monster inside its borders will be instantly annihilated. Simple, no?"

From the way he was looking at us, he actually seemed to believe that. I wondered if he even knew what the word *simple* meant.

"I do," he assured me.

I shot Nero an apologetic glance for thinking in front of a god—again. Well, maybe I was only half-sorry. It wasn't my fault I liked to think.

Ronan's gaze shifted to me, his eyes a storm of black, silver, and gold. "In your short time at the Legion, you have acquired quite the reputation."

"For causing trouble?"

"Yes. And for fixing trouble."

"I will endeavor to do that here. Uh, fix trouble. Not cause it." I smiled at him.

"I know you will."

I wasn't sure if his words were a compliment or a threat. I did know that his stormy eyes made every hair on my body stand up in terror, so I redirected my gaze elsewhere. I looked over the bronze-accented edge of the airship, down to the lands below.

The Western Wilderness was hot, scorched. A wild city sat on the forsaken desert. That must have been the City of Ashes. It looked centuries old. The desert's red sands had rolled over the city, burying parts of it. At the city's edge, empty building husks howled a forlorn song from a forgotten era. But the wall around the city did, in fact, seem to be intact. No, not just intact. It looked brand-spanking new. It was as though it were immune to the passage of time. There wasn't a single hole in it. That was weird.

There was no moon out tonight, only thick clouds that hung over the city like a blanket of ash. A shrill, feral howl sang on the wind. It sounded like a werewolf, but worse. It was something much, much scarier—the savage scream of a monstrous beast that ate civilization for breakfast. A chorus of similar howls, just as savage, answered its call, adding their cries to the wind. There had to be dozens of them down there, each one probably as big as a house. And as mean as a hound of hell.

Nero had told me that the monsters hadn't been pretty to begin with, back in the days when they'd first attacked the Earth. And they'd only gotten worse since. They'd become twisted and corrupted by the wild magic here, interbreeding to create even more terrifying beasts. Down there, in the City of Ashes, the nightmarish monsters reigned supreme. Thousands of tiny lights shone out from the shadows. The city had no power, no magic illumination. Those tiny lights were the eyes of the beasts who lived there.

Simple? That's what Ronan had said. I didn't buy it. Nero's trials would be as simple as wrestling a dinosaur with our bare hands. Or riding a shark naked. Or… I stopped the next ridiculous image before it formed in my head. I was supposed to be masking my thoughts better.

"Call me when the job is done," Ronan told Nero.

The statement was loaded with meaning. He was letting us know that we weren't leaving the City of Ashes until the Magitech barrier was back up. And if we failed—if we died here— the sands would roll over our bodies, burying us in the wilderness.

A small box appeared in Ronan's hands, as though it had materialized out of thin air. Hell, it probably had. He opened the lid. Inside lay two small vials filled with inky liquid.

"This is the potion that will mute your magic," Ronan

explained. "It will silence your most recent gift from the gods. Then it will take a power from you every few minutes until you have no magic left."

I looked at the two vials in Ronan's hands. The liquid was moving, oozing, glistening in an eerie way, like it was alive. But that was ridiculous. It certainly was not alive. I was letting my fear—fear of what that potion would do to me— get the better of me. Yes, I was afraid. I could admit that. I hadn't had my magic for very long, but it had become a part of me. The thought of it being stripped away, of losing a piece of who I was, even if it was just for a short while, was downright terrifying. I might as well have been going into battle naked.

"You are supposed to be afraid," Ronan said, responding to my turbulent thoughts. "And vulnerable. These trials test what kind of angel you are inside, without your magic." He looked at me as he spoke, those godly eyes changing, shimmering like pure gold.

"I am not an angel," I said.

"Nyx has high hopes for you." His gaze shifted to Nero. "For both of you. So don't screw it up." He handed us the vials.

My heart thumped even as I held my vial, staring into its swirling, silvery depths. I knew it was cowardly to fear the loss of my magic. I just didn't want to be weak again. I wanted to run away, to protect my magic with everything I had.

But I had to be brave. I had to be there for Nero when he needed me, just like he'd always been there for me. There was no fear on his face. I didn't even feel it through our bond. He was so strong. I owed it to him to be strong too. He'd chosen me to help him in this important test, picked me over stronger, more experienced soldiers. I refused to be the weak link. I refused to let him down.

"Cheers," I said with a small smile, raising my vial.

We clinked glasses and drank. The potion poured down my throat like liquid ice, chilling me. It felt like I'd just swallowed the Arctic. A wintery storm took root inside of me, freezing my blood, making it flow as slow as molasses.

Beside me, Nero clenched his fists, shattering the empty vial. He didn't shake. He was as solid as a mountain. But I could feel something now—a profound sense of loss, as though a piece of him had been ripped away.

I shivered, my hands shaking as I dropped the vial. I felt cold—so very cold. My elemental magic felt muted, cut off. My pulse raced, my mind panicking as I tallied off all the other magic I still had to lose. Siren's Song. Witch's Cauldron. Vampire's Kiss. And then, at the end, I would be mortal again. Weak again.

I was hit with the overwhelming urge to run away and hide myself. A tiny sane part of my mind reminded me that there was no hiding from this. It was too late. I had already drunk the potion. My magic would abandon me. The only way to get it back was to see this through.

Somehow, that wasn't the least bit comforting.

"Good," Ronan said, looking at us. "Very good."

Then he lifted his hands. A blast of psychic energy tore out of them. His magic slammed into us like a hammer, knocking us over the side of the airship.

4

THE CITY OF ASHES

I fell down to the City of Ashes. I couldn't see Nero. The raging sandstorm had pushed us apart. My eyes watered, my throat burned, and my heart was galloping so hard that it was a wonder it hadn't burst through my chest. Through the swirling wind funnels, I could hardly see more than a few feet in front of me.

I dropped through the whirlwind of sand and smoke, and then I could see again. The old city was right below me —and the ground was coming fast. Past the city's borders, far in the distance, I saw the golden glow of the Magitech barrier that separated the wild lands from human civilization in the west. The barrier around the city itself, the old final line of defense, was out. It didn't glow with that distinctive gold magic. It looked so sad, so empty, so forlorn.

A piercing screech cried out from above me. Monsters— giant black birds—circled over the city. There were two of them, each the size of a large Legion truck. On the ground, they would have towered over me. Here in the air, I felt even smaller. I was the tiny worm they fed to their monstrous young.

6

The birds screeched again and dove for me. They were so close that I could see the murderous gleam in their eyes. Those eyes! They were blacker than their feathers, blacker than the bottomless abyss.

I was dropping fast with no way to slow my fall—and no way to fight the monsters. I had no elemental magic. The potions I had on me weren't potent enough to take out something that big. And my vampiric strength and speed were of zero use to me during a free-fall. I reached out with my siren's magic to compel the beastly birds, but their minds were too strong, too intent on eating me. I couldn't override the primal instincts of the hunt. Nero had always warned me that it was easiest to take control of a beast's mind when it was caught unawares.

It was just as well. The gods were watching, and if they found out I had some power over the beasts that they themselves had lost control over, they would try to figure out why. Finding out would surely involve turning me into a human pincushion, which was a fate I'd prefer to avoid.

The birds screeched, their cries so close that my eardrums rang. In a few seconds, I would be bird food.

A gust of wind punched through the air, knocking the birds off course. No, it wasn't the wind. It was Nero. He flew past the birds, his dark wings beating fast. Blasts of telekinetic energy shot out of his hands, tossing the beasts aside. He swooped under me and caught me.

"Got you," he said.

I breathed a sigh of relief.

"Don't celebrate yet." As he dove straight down toward the city, my heart jumped.

The beastly birds had already recovered. They were closing in on us fast. And they were spitting fire. Nero zigzagged through the air, dodging the flames.

And then I felt it—another flash of cold, like jumping into an icy ocean. Ronan's potion was striking again, chipping away at my magic once more. For me, that meant the power of Siren's Song. But for Nero… We shook and dropped. Oh, shit. Soon, he wouldn't be able to use his angel magic anymore. He wouldn't be able to fly.

He recovered from the drop, steadying us. But I couldn't help but notice that his wings were beating more slowly now. They weren't strong enough to hold my weight.

"You have to let me go," I told him.

He held stubbornly to me. "I am not sacrificing you."

"Believe me, I don't want to be sacrificed either. Without me, you'll never survive this test." I struggled to keep the smirk on my lips—and the panic out of my voice. "Toss me up to that bird." I pointed at the shadow of the beast flying above us, blacking out the stars in the sky.

"I am not using you as a weapon."

"This is the only way. Your wings are fading. You need to trust me, Nero."

He met my eyes for a long moment, then he tossed me. As I shot up toward the giant bird, I prayed that it didn't move out of the way. I was betting on the beast's arrogance, its confidence as an alpha predator. I used what was left of my siren magic to get into its head, to control the beast—not to fight its instincts, but to work with them. To feed its ego.

Nero was right. I couldn't force beasts to do things they didn't want to—with the notable exception of that herd on the Elemental Plains, the monsters engineered to be a perfect mix of light and dark magic. However, I could use the monsters' own wicked natures against them. I could feed the predator instinct, the beasts' feelings of superiority, their arrogance.

The bird didn't dodge out of my way. As I collided with

it, I grabbed onto its back, my fingers digging through the glossy black feathers, clawing deep to the skin beneath. The bird shook with shock and anger. It bucked hard, trying to throw me off. I clung to it, grabbing fists of feathers, just trying to hold on.

Ice froze my blood—and my breath. I felt the last of my siren magic leave me. The magic slipped through my fingers like oil. And then it was gone.

I held onto the bird. My magic was abandoning me, but my stubbornness would not fade. My time at the Legion hadn't just grown my magic and combat skills. I'd become stronger inside. That was what Nero had taught me.

Oh, no, Nero.

I looked down, searching for him. My siren magic was gone. That meant his angel power was gone too. I found him. His wings had disappeared. No longer an angel, he was free-falling down to the ground.

The bird I was riding saw him too. It dove for him, opening its mouth to shoot fire. The other bird was flying in from the other side of Nero. The two beasts were in a hot race to eat him first.

We weren't far now from the city's upper peaks. I kicked and pulled with all my strength, turning my bird as it opened its mouth. It shrieked in pain and swerved into the other bird. I jumped off the beast and grabbed Nero, knocking us onto a rooftop. Above us, the two birds collided in a fiery explosion. Wow, they sure had a lot of fire in them.

I shot Nero a crooked smile. "Got you."

He looked over the edge of the building; a few more inches and we'd have missed the roof and fallen to our deaths. Then he looked up at the burning black feathers raining down on us and chuckled.

"What?" I demanded.

"I really did pick the perfect name for you, Pandora."

"I'm glad you find this all so amusing. Now how about we climb down to the ground before some other beastie decides we'd make a good snack."

"Agreed."

We hadn't made it even halfway down to the ground when another cold flash hit me. My next ability abandoned me, the power of witchcraft. I couldn't mix a potion now if my life depended on it—which, down here, it probably did. Even if I could have remembered the spells now trapped behind a thick, impenetrable curtain in my mind, I didn't have the magic to mix them. I couldn't infuse life into the mixture. And without that magical spark, the potions were nothing more than glorified vitamin drinks.

But there was nothing I could do about any of that. I just had to keep going. Keep climbing. I stole a glance at the city —at the ruins, the decay, the broken barrier that we were supposed to fix. Somehow. The city looked so old in some places and yet so new in others. The monsters' magic, the magic of the wilds, was a mystery. Sometimes, the wild lands took over quickly. Sometimes, their magic moved at a snail's pace. The wild magic was unpredictable, uncontrollable. And dangerous. Most of all, it was dangerous.

Most of the decay was at the city's borders. The inner sections appeared mainly untouched. The weather was just as chaotic. Hot, wild sandstorms raged along the eastern edge of the city, but the air was cooling fast as the sun's final rays faded from the darkening sky. The sandstorm was becoming a blizzard. Tiny snowflakes fell onto the scorching sand. A layer of white flakes coated the ground. For some reason, it didn't even melt.

Weather and magic were completely out of sync on the plains of monsters. Not long ago, the angel Colonel Leila

Starborn had conducted magical experiments to correct the bizarre weather in the wilds. Maybe if she'd succeeded, she could have put the magic of the wild areas back into sync with the rest of the world.

Nero and I touched down on the ground. Sweat drenched his body, and I didn't think it was from our climb down the building. This was Ronan's potion at work. His muscles twitched. He looked weaker than I'd ever seen him.

"Are you all right?" I asked him.

"I must admit, after two centuries with my magic, it's been quite a shock to my body to lose it. And to my mind."

"I don't feel so great myself."

"You look almost normal. You are strong." Admiration shone in his eyes.

"I don't feel strong. I feel sick and weak. My head feels like it's going to explode, and my stomach is twisted into a hard knot."

"You are still on your feet. You're handling it better than I am."

"I guess it helps that I lived most of my life without magic. Losing it was not as big of a shock to my system as it was to yours." I planted a big smile over the gaping hole inside of me where my magic used to be.

Nero wasn't fooled. "The loss of that much magic is always a shock, Leda. You are handling it not because the effects of the potion are weaker on you. You are handling it because you are strong." He set his hands on my shoulders and kissed my forehead. "And I need you to stay strong."

A short burst of pain trickled through our bond, and then it was gone.

"You," I gasped. "You've been blocking me. You don't want me to feel what you're feeling."

31

"It's better this way. I will not burden you with my weakness."

I grabbed his hand and set it on my heart, a heart that ached for him. "Don't hide it, Nero. Don't hold it back. We're in this together. Let me take some of your pain."

"I cannot ask that of you."

"You're not asking me. I'm telling you. We're stronger together."

"Are you sure?"

"That I'm right?" I grinned at him. "Of course. I'm always right. I thought you'd realized that by now."

But Nero didn't laugh. He lifted his hand to my cheek.

Agony lashed out at me, cutting through my body. My legs gave out. The pain filled the wretched emptiness inside of me. Hot and cold, fire and ice—it boiled higher and higher, drowning me, swallowing me, consuming me. I couldn't see, couldn't hear, couldn't speak. I could barely breathe. There was nothing but the pain. I knew with horrible, undeniable certainty that it would never end. I would never be free of this torment—not as long as I lived.

Leda!

There was only one way to end it. Death was an escape. The pain could not follow me there.

I can't block it off. You have to fight it!

Nero?

I grabbed onto the sound of his voice, focusing on that tiny beacon of hope in a sea of despair. I could almost see him now. The pain lessened to a dull, constant ache.

"Leda." His voice wasn't only in my head now.

"I'm all right now," I croaked, my vision clearing. The first thing I saw was his face. "I was just caught off guard. I…" I choked back tears. "I didn't realize your pain was so…so…"

He touched my face. "I should never have let you feel that." Frustration crinkled his forehead. "Now that I opened our connection, I can't seem to close it."

"Don't try to close it." I set my hand on his. "I can handle it." I smiled at him. "I can hardly feel it anymore."

"Leda, you don't need to pretend with me. I know exactly what you are feeling."

Like my soul had been shredded apart, then stuck back together with sticky tape.

"We're in this together," I told him. "And I'm not arguing with you. Yes, it hurts, and it sucks. If you really want us both to stop feeling this, then let's fix the Magitech barrier and get the hell out of here. Where do we begin?"

"We will start with your cuts and burns," he said.

I cringed as his finger pulled back the scorched corners of the big hole in my jacket.

"Didn't anyone ever tell you that it's reckless to jump off of monstrous, fire-breathing birds?"

I put on a sassy smirk. "I distinctly remember you only warned me to stay away from giant thunder birds, not fire-breathing ones."

Nero sighed. "You shouldn't have shielded me from the fire with your body. My magic is stronger. You should have allowed me to shield you."

"Nero Windstriker, let's just get one thing straight. I might have lost most of my magic, but I am not useless. I don't need magic to be a human shield."

He set his hand on my arm, then he jerked back, like he'd been shocked. "I can't heal you. I've lost that magic." He looked so helpless, so lost, but he covered those emotions quickly. "I'll use a potion."

He reached into the potion pouches on his belt. He pulled out three vials—then he just stopped.

33

"Nero?"

"I can't remember the spell." He spun around and blasted away a pile of rocks in frustration.

"Are you finished?" I asked him.

"Yes."

"Feel better?"

"A little," he admitted.

Laughter burst out of my mouth.

"This is not funny, Leda."

But I couldn't stop laughing. Maybe I'd finally lost my mind.

"Are you finished?" he asked me.

I swallowed a final chuckle. "Yes."

"Feel better?"

"A little."

His lower lip twitched, and though no laughter escaped him, I could feel him laughing inside.

"Let me see your potion pouches," I said, holding out my hand.

He detached them from his belt and handed them to me.

I peeked inside the pouches. "You can use the lavender and lily water to make a salve for the burns."

"How do you know? Is Ronan's potion not affecting you completely?"

He meant because I had light and dark magic.

"No, it's affecting me completely. It's blocked out the magic I gained from Nectar and Venom, light and dark," I replied. "But I knew this recipe before I joined the Legion, before I drank the Nectar of the gods. My sister Bella used to make it for us all the time. I just don't have the magic to mix it myself."

Nero quickly mixed the two ingredients into a thick

paste, which he spread across my burns. I breathed out in relief as my burnt skin cooled.

"I wish I could truly heal you," Nero said.

Unlike many of the Legion's favorite battlefield balms, this one wasn't potent enough to heal my wounds instantly, but it did take away my pain.

"Hey, don't worry about it. I'm a tough girl."

"My blood would heal you."

"I'm not going to drink from you, Nero. That would weaken you. I can manage."

"Are you sure?"

"Yes. It doesn't hurt any more than training with you." I smirked at him.

"Don't be cute with me, Pandora."

"I'd never dream of it, Colonel."

He made a gruff noise that might have been a snort. "The Magitech generators should be in there." He pointed at the brick building across the street.

"Great," I said brightly as we headed for the power building. "Let's give them a power boost, get the barrier back up, and then get the hell out of here. This will be easy. I bet we can get it done in record time, well before you lose all your magic. The gods will be so impressed. In addition to promoting you, they'll grant you any favor you want."

"Grant me any favor I want? Obviously, you don't know the gods very well."

I gave my hand a dismissive wave. "Don't be a party pooper, Colonel Hardass."

His brows lifted. "Colonel Hardass?"

"Just a little nickname that Ivy and I used to call you when we first joined the Legion, way back when you were making our lives a living hell."

"I had no idea you took an interest in my ass so early on in our relationship."

"Relationship? The only relationship we had back then was of torturer and trainee. I hated you with every aching fiber of my being."

The grin Nero gave me was almost evil. "I knew you'd come around eventually."

"How could you possibly know that?" I demanded.

"You have a dangerous habit of always trying to see the best in everyone. Even in angels. And I am a patient man."

"Oh, you were plotting to win me over, were you? You must have realized that pushups are the surest way to a girl's heart."

"Your training was completely independent of any intentions I might have had."

I gave him my most skeptical look.

"All right. My intentions might not have been entirely honorable. Especially when I was sitting on you while you were doing pushups," he admitted.

"Ha! I knew it! You should be ashamed of yourself, Colonel." I shook my head. "Seducing a sweet, young initiate with promises of pushups."

"I'm crying inside."

I snorted. "I'm sure."

"If it makes you feel better, next time you can sit on me while I'm doing pushups," he said with a sly smile.

Heat scorched my cheeks. I didn't know why I blushed, but I knew it was all his fault.

"So," I said. "When the gods grant you a boon for your stellar performance here…" I stopped when his lower lip twitched in amusement. "What's so funny?"

"The gods don't grant boons, Pandora."

"Thinking is being. Be positive." I slapped him on the

back. "You could ask for your old job back. Then you'd come back to New York and kick Harker out of your office." I grinned at him. "We'll do it together. It will be fun."

Nero stopped and stroked his hand down my face.

"What is it?" I asked.

"Nothing." His mouth brushed against my neck.

I blushed—again. "What if the gods are watching?" I couldn't see them, but that didn't mean they weren't watching us. In fact, I was pretty sure they were.

"Let them watch."

His words were as smooth as honey, as decadent as silk. And when he kissed me, heat poured out of his mouth, igniting my blood, burning away the cold ice of the gods' potion. I dug my nails into the hard muscle of his back, drawing him in closer.

He pulled away, breaking off the kiss. "Later," he whispered against my ear.

"I'm going to hold you to that."

"I'd be disappointed if you didn't," he replied.

"I'd hate to disappoint an angel. You angels are such a moody bunch."

"Yes." Gold flashed in his eyes. "We are." His face grew serious again. "We need to get to the Magitech generators and fix them before I lose the power of witchcraft. This test was designed to challenge me, so we can be sure that restarting these generators won't be easy. I will need all the technical knowledge and magic I have left."

"So if we don't hurry, we might not have the knowledge and magic to be able to fix the generators?"

"Yes."

"Well," I said, swallowing hard. "On the bright side, none of that will matter if the monsters eat us."

I pointed at the giant spider headed our way.

37

5

HUMAN AGAIN

*G*iant was perhaps an inadequate word to describe the monster closing in on us. Enormous? Gargantuan? Colossal? None of those words captured the horror of staring down a spider twice my size. As black as tar, it glistened and gleamed like a pool of oil in the rising moonlight. The wind was agitated, buzzing, rustling. When the beast moved, it sounded like the sharpening of a hundred knives at once.

"That is a highly poisonous spider," Nero told me.

Of course it was. As though I'd ever doubted it. This place was hell on Earth.

The spider rushed us, slashing out with its pointy-tipped legs. Each slash whistled through the air like a steel sword. They cut like a sword too.

"That spider moves really fast for a beast its size," I said, ignoring the throbbing pain in my left shoulder where the beast had cut me.

We struck at the giant spider with our swords. Our blades scraped against the beast's belly, hardly scratching the hard shell. It was like hitting a shield.

The spider reared back and ejected a white bundle of goo. I ducked out of the way, and the web shot past me, splattering against a nearby building. It stuck right where it had hit. I couldn't afford to let the spider trap me in its web. Or poison me with those shiny silver pinchers.

I considered going around the beast to get to the Magitech generator building, but another spider jumped into my path—and this one was even larger than the first. Nero went to greet the new arrival, leaving me to battle the first spider.

My spider rushed forward, slashing with its hard, armored legs as it ejected another sticky white bundle. I ducked low to avoid the web. Then I grabbed the beast's leg with both hands and heaved with as much power as I had. The leg crunched, cracking into two in my hands. The spider fell.

It tried to get back up, but with a leg missing it was a circling, panicking, horribly uncoordinated mess. It snapped and hissed at me, shooting out bundles of stinking white goo, one after the other. The damn thing was a machine gun.

I rolled under the spider and jumped up, shoving my sword through its open jaws. My blade sank into the soft inner flesh of its mouth and pierced the top of its head. The lights went out in those hellish eyes, then it dropped dead to the ground. A moment later, Nero's spider landed on its body. It was dead too. I looked at the pile of spiders, and I had to admit I was feeling pretty damn badass.

That victory song died in my head when I saw the stream of giant spiders flying down every building in sight. There were dozens of them, and every single one of them was determined to eat us alive. Nero blasted one of them off the building with a psychic spell. The spider fell dead to the ground. So they were weak against magic. Unfortunately,

Nero and I were a bit short on magic right now. His spells weren't nearly as strong as they used to be.

A cold, foreboding flash shook my body, a silent tremor that warned me of the larger quake to come. Soon my vampire powers would leave me completely, and then I would be as weak and slow as a human. I wouldn't be able to fight off the spiders in that state. I would be a liability. I *hated* being a liability, especially to Nero. He wouldn't be strong enough to kill them all alone if he had to worry about saving my human ass.

Nero pummeled the spiders with psychic energy, one blast after the other. He didn't slow down, but I could see the strain in his face. He was weakening. His magic was not as potent as he needed for this battle. I'd always thought Nero was a bottomless well of stamina, but watching him fight those beasts now, I could see his limits. He wouldn't hold out for much longer.

The quake came—and it didn't come gently. It tore away the last of my magic, leaving me weak. Mortal. Beside me, Nero groaned in pain, my loss magnified by his own. I could feel his anguish, like a hammer had slammed down on him, shattering him. A tear slid from my eye. And at that moment, I realized that I wasn't just carrying his burden; he was carrying mine. He felt everything that I did, and it hurt him.

So I bottled up my thoughts, my pain, everything.

"So that's what it takes for you to reel in your thoughts," Nero joked, but the smile didn't reach his eyes.

We looked up at the sky of spiders. His psychic magic gone, he waved his hand to create a lightning whip. The most powerful Legion soldiers didn't even need a weapon. They could form one out of pure magic.

"Wait," I said as he prepared to strike out at the

monsters. "I have a better idea. Right now the spiders are on tons of buildings." I pointed at the ugly concrete building in front of us. "But if we could lure them all to one place…"

"We could get them all at once," he finished for me.

"Exactly. Once they are all on that building, you need to electrocute the whole thing."

He looked at the building, then at me. "You are not drawing them to that building. You will get electrocuted too."

"I'm tough. I'll be ok."

"No," he said stubbornly. "I'm not using you as bait."

"I have no magic, no supernatural strength. I can't take down even one of them. I can only be bait. That's the only way I can help."

He stepped in front of me. "I will take care of them myself. I have enough magic left for that."

"You probably do. But these aren't the first monsters we've faced here, and they won't be the last. If you burn out now, you won't have enough magic left later. This is a marathon, Nero." A sick, deadly marathon orchestrated by the gods. "You have to pace yourself." I set my hand on his arm. "We can do this. Together. You have to trust me. This isn't the time for prim and proper fighting. To survive this, you're going to have to fight a little dirty."

When Nero opened his mouth to protest, I grabbed a handful of sand from the ground and threw it in his face. Then, not looking back, I ran toward the building.

"That wasn't funny, Pandora," he called out between coughs.

I kept running. My lungs burned, my feet felt like lead—and I was hardly moving at all. I'd sure taken my supernatural speed for granted.

"Come and get me!" I screamed at the spiders as loudly as I could.

Their heads all turned toward me, frozen for a moment in time. Their red eyes shone like hundreds of little lights. I slashed my knife across my arm and flicked it, sprinkling the sand with my blood. The spiders unfroze and stampeded toward me.

I ran into the building and slammed the door shut behind me. The walls shook and trembled. The spiders were crashing their hard, armored bodies against the building. They tore at the windows, the door, the holes in the walls—anything to get inside. Bits of glass, concrete, and brick rained down on me. Noxious green smoke, smelling of burning metal and acid, rose from the webs they splatted against the building. The noise of it all was awful, simply wretched. It sounded like a metal workshop, a power saw, and a horror house—punctuated with the sound of someone's head hitting a gym mat over and over again. The spiders were almost inside. Parts of their legs had already broken through the walls.

Ribbons of purple lightning blasted across the building, shooting up level by level. The magic covered every wall, spilled through every window. The stink of burning flesh overwhelmed the blend of metal and acid. Spiders dropped dead to the ground like black rain.

I ran for the exit, grabbing a wooden board from the ground. I slammed the board against the door, but the spiders' web had sealed it shut. I kept hammering the door, but it wouldn't budge.

I tossed the useless board aside. There was a broken window nearby. I sprinted toward it and jumped through. I landed hard on a dead spider on the other side, slipping over its sleek body.

I peeled my face off the dirt. Nero stood over me, the last remnants of lightning fading from his hands. He shook off the magic, then extended his hand to help me up. He looked from the damaged building, to the piles of dead giant spiders.

Then he looked at me and said, "Don't you ever do that again."

I smirked at him. "I told you it would work."

A dead spider fell off the roof of the building. Nero picked me up and swept me out of the way. Had he moved a second later, the monster's corpse would have crushed me.

"Bringer of Chaos." He tucked a stray strand of hair behind my ear.

I grinned at him. "Admit it. Your life was boring before me. You'd always yearned for a healthy dose of chaos in your life."

Nero fell to his knees, his face contorted with pain. Through our bond, I could feel his magic fading.

"Are you all right?" I asked.

"I've lost my ability to shift."

I wiped black spider blood from my sleeve. "That's ok. We can practice Shifter's Shadow later."

As soon as I said it, I realized how stupid it was. I shouldn't have been worrying about my training for the fifth level right now, when we were in a fight for our lives. I didn't even have magic right now. Ronan's potion hadn't just taken out my magic; it had muddled my mind. I guess that was kind of the point of the trials: to strip us of everything and set us loose in this fallen city.

Nero set his hand on my arm. "Come on. The power building is just next door."

I followed him inside. The building looked mostly intact. Old, but mostly intact. There wasn't even much rust, certainly not as much as you'd expect to find after two centuries of neglect. Several of the nearby buildings were nothing but rust. The laws of nature were way out of whack here.

We stepped into darkness. Nero pulled out a Witch Lantern, a potion-powered lamp. The golden light shone out like a star, illuminating the tall, open hallway. As we followed the path, I could have sworn I saw things moving in the shadows. Maybe I was imagining things, but I didn't think so. This city had been overrun by monsters. They were everywhere. That didn't mean whatever was watching us right now would attack. There were all kinds of monsters, including timid ones.

"Here we are," Nero said as we reached a cylinder the size of a barn.

I wondered how they'd gotten it into the building.

"I'm going to see what we're dealing with." He lifted the lamp up to the Magitech generator.

As he looked it over, I kept an eye out for beasties. A few minutes later, he stepped around the generator, his expression masked.

"Is this the point where you tell me you have good news and bad news?" I quipped.

"There's a small amount of magic left in the generator," he told me.

"That was the good news?"

"There is no good news, Pandora. We have a much bigger problem. The magic in the generators has been corrupted by the monsters' wild magic. And the city's barrier isn't broken. It's perfectly intact. In fact, it's still connected to the continent's barrier system."

"And that's bad?"

"The corrupted magic is bleeding through that connection, into the larger grid. The city's generator is very slowly infecting all the others. The barriers that protect the cities of humanity from the plains of monsters are breaking down. If we don't fix the problem and purge the wild magic, every barrier on the continent will come down, opening the door for monsters to flood the cities."

6

MAGICAL MACHINATIONS

I stood beside the barn-sized Magitech power generator, counting the dust bunnies on the floor. There were some brick bunnies and glass bunnies too. If I got lucky, none of them would spontaneously come to life. Stranger things had been known to happen on the plains of monsters.

Nero was talking on his phone to Ronan. He had it on speakerphone so I could hear too. Eavesdropping was so much harder with human hearing.

"The generator is bleeding corrupted power into the main barrier system," Nero reported to the Lord of the Legion. "When the barrier around the city fell long ago, this generator—this part of the wall—was never properly cut off from the other barriers on the continent."

I considered how we'd gotten into this situation. The Magitech barriers were connected throughout the continent in a grid so the whole barrier system could have consistent power, so they could be controlled together. But this efficiency had created the problem we were facing right now. In their arrogance, the gods had never dreamed that even a single barrier would fail.

The Magitech and designs the gods had given humanity were truly powerful. There was no denying that. So what had happened in the City of Ashes? It must have been something truly catastrophic if it brought down the city's barrier. A saboteur attacking from the inside? I'd have to ask Nero later. I knew nothing of the events that had transpired here. There was nothing in the history books. In fact, I'd never even heard of the City of Ashes before Nero and Ronan had spoken of it on the airship. The gods must have wanted to bury any and all evidence that they were not infallible.

"It is a slow bleed of magic, a slow contamination, but it is growing," Nero told Ronan. "We might have months before the continent's barriers go down, or it might be a matter of hours. We need to send in an engineering team to come fix it before the whole system goes down and the monsters overrun every city in North America."

Nero paused, waiting for Ronan to respond. The hiss and pop of the line echoed in the room. Finally, the God of War spoke.

"This turn of events is most disturbing," he said. "Now more than ever before, it's important that you complete your mission and save this city. This is no longer merely about your test; it's about humanity's very survival. I trust you will perform admirably, Colonel Windstriker."

And with that said, Ronan hung up.

Nero put away his phone. He looked stunned. And it took a lot to stun Nero.

"I cannot believe what I just heard," I said. "The world is at stake, and they are doing nothing?"

The gods weren't always nice, but they did want to protect the Earth. Even if it was only for their own interests, whatever those were, they wouldn't allow the barriers to fall. They wouldn't allow civilization to fall into chaos.

Nero was quiet for a moment, looking thoughtful. Then he said, "This is the test."

"What?"

"This isn't a turn of events," he said. "This is staged. All of it. Planned down to the last detail. This is all playing out exactly as the gods planned."

"They knew about the danger to the continent's barriers?"

"They not only knew about it. I believe they created the issue."

I blinked. "But that's insane. Surely the gods would not risk every city on the continent—so many lives—for a test."

"They would."

"That's so…heartless."

"That is the way of the gods, Leda. We are all players in their game. These are their rules."

I struggled to put words to what I was feeling. Anger, betrayal, outrage, desperation, hopelessness, vengeance. My feelings tore me in a hundred different directions at once.

Nero set his hands on my shoulders. "Getting upset won't save anyone. We need to stop the spread of the contaminated magic."

"How?"

"The contaminated magic is weak. It's a broken mixture of a dozen different wild magics from the monsters who have taken over the city. It has no strength, no harmony. If we flood the city's Magitech generator with pure magic, it will wash away the corruption."

"So how do we do that?"

"We need to jolt the generator back to life."

Nero faced the generator and took a deep breath, slowly swinging his hands over his head. Lightning sizzled on his fingertips. He drew in another deep breath, then he blasted the generator with magic. It rumbled, like it was starting up, but then it stuttered out.

"I don't have enough magic," Nero said, his voice monotone.

Pain flashed across our connection. Ronan's potion took this opportune moment to kick him while he was down, ripping the elemental magic away from him. I caught him as he fell. I nearly fell too, my knees buckling under his weight—and the strain of our connection. I felt the turmoil, the pain, the sense of failure—every horrible thing that he felt, as though it were my pain. As though it were my turmoil. It felt like being burned alive.

Nero recovered his balance. He glared at the snoring generator and declared, "It didn't work."

"That would have been too easy. These trials were designed to be tough for us."

"Yes." He let out a hard, humorless laugh. "They stripped me of the power I need to solve the problem. Of course they would not make the answer be so simple. But what is the answer? How can we fix this?"

Something tugged at my senses. I feared it was the next wave coming to take my magic away, but then I remembered I had no more magic left to take. This was something else. Something familiar buzzed inside my head. A noise. No, not a noise. A feeling. A presence. For some reason, it reminded me of Damiel, Nero's father.

I was probably just imagining things. Damiel had offered to help Nero prepare for the Gods' Trials. Nero, stubborn angel that he was, had refused. And now my mind was wondering what would have happened if he'd taken Damiel's help.

You would have been prepared, the voice said. Damiel's voice.

But Damiel was back in New York. Telepathic magic or not, he couldn't speak to me from there.

Yes, I can.

Fantastic. The stress was finally cracking me. I was not only hearing voices in my head; I was talking to them too. I'd officially lost my mind.

Why do people who hear voices inside their head always assume they're crazy?

Not now, Damiel. We are in the middle of a crisis.

Nero gave me a strange look.

"What?" I asked.

He tapped his forehead.

He can hear me too, Damiel told me.

Nero nodded.

So I'm not crazy?

No, you're still crazy, Leda. But take solace in the fact that you're not the only one.

The room faded before my eyes, swallowed by thick fog. A high-pitched ding chimed in the distance.

"A waking trance," Nero said.

"Waking trance?"

"Damiel has put us in it."

"Why?"

"That is a good question." Nero looked around. "Do you recognize this place?"

The distant ding grew less distant, more defined. It sounded like a carousel melody. The fog cleared a little, revealing a carnival. Colorful lights flashed in front of rides and games. A pile of stuffed toy unicorns was stacked behind one of the stalls.

"This is the carnival that stops near Purgatory every

summer," I said. "Calli brought us here a bunch of times when we were kids." I picked up one of the toy unicorns.

"A unicorn?" Nero asked.

"One summer, I won a few of them for me and my sisters."

His brows arched in amusement.

"What? I like unicorns. They're pretty."

The fog rolled aside to reveal Damiel, one of the scariest angels who'd ever lived. And he was holding a fluffy pink unicorn in his arms.

"What is this all about?" Nero demanded. "What are we doing here? What are *you* doing here?"

"This is Leda's mind. We are inside one of her lovely memories." Damiel pointed at a young teenage me standing at one of the games, shooting metal cans with a slingshot.

"We don't have time for this," Nero told him.

"Indeed. There is little time," Damiel agreed. "We must move quickly. I am using your connection to Leda to speak to you both."

"You're Nero's father. How are we in my mind?" I asked him.

"I am connected to you through Nero. Whether he likes it or not, he is my son, and that too is a bond forged in magic."

"But why my mind instead of Nero's?"

"I chose your mind because right now your powers are cut off; your connection to the gods is severed. They cannot see or hear us here. We can speak freely," said Damiel. "I'm sure you've realized by now that the gods' potion does not affect the magic of your bond."

Yeah, I had noticed that. And wondered about it.

"Such bonds are forged with a different kind of magic. It

is an ancient magic that does not come from the gods' Nectar —or from the demons' Venom."

"Damiel, this is all very fascinating, but I doubt you came here to talk about ancient magic. Do you know what is happening here?"

He smiled at me. "Straight to the point as always. Yes, I am aware of your situation."

"Can you help us?" I asked.

"We are not cheating," Nero told me.

I sighed. "Nero, when the world is at stake, you are allowed to cheat."

"Says who?"

"Says me."

"We will find a way ourselves."

Gods, the man was stubborn.

"We don't have much time," I told him. "The barriers will fail, and the monsters will flood every city on the continent. We cannot allow all of those people to die. Our friends. Our family."

Nero looked at me. "We will find a way. We always do."

"Don't waste your breath, dear," Damiel said to me. "Nero is too stubborn to accept my help."

"Your help always comes at a price." Nero folded his arms across his chest. "You always have an agenda."

Damiel smiled. "Perhaps. But let's not fool ourselves, Nero. So do you. You are your father's son."

Nero clenched his teeth.

"I'm glad you and Leda have bonded," said Damiel. "She is a good influence on you."

The bond. That was it!

"Right now, neither of us has much magic, but our bond is magical," I said.

Damiel nodded. "Bonds between souls require a spark of

light or dark magic to ignite. But the bond itself is woven with an ancient magic that the gods' potion cannot smother." He looked between me and Nero and said, "Yours is a particularly strong bond."

"If we used the magic from our bond, would that be enough magic to start the generators and save everyone?" I asked.

"Indeed it would," said Damiel.

"Leda…" Nero's face was hard, but his eyes were as turbulent as a storm at sea.

Guilt crashed and turned inside of me. I'd hurt his feelings. He thought I was throwing away our connection.

"We could make it again, our bond, when we have our magic back," I said quickly.

"Interesting," Damiel commented.

"Enough," Nero growled at Damiel. He looked at me, his tone a tad softer, "You too, Pandora."

Despair ripped across our bond. Nero tried to hold it back, but it was like a tsunami slamming against the barriers of his mind—and his heart. This was my fault. I shouldn't have suggested it. Our bond meant something to him. It meant something to me too. But if we could remake the bond, would it be worth sacrificing it for a short time to save millions of lives? I'd thought so when I'd suggested it, but now I just didn't know. I reached for Nero, trying to comfort him.

Nero recoiled from my touch. "This is what they want." He glared at Damiel. "Isn't it?"

"Yes."

Nero's gaze shifted to me. "This is why she's here."

"Yes," Damiel said again.

The floodgates of our bond opened, and the tsunami crashed against me, drowning me in Nero's agony. I'd never felt anything like it, not even when he'd lost his magic. I didn't understand the tears streaming down my cheeks. I only knew that my heart was in pieces, and I'd never feel whole again.

"What is it?" I asked Nero, choking on my tears.

Anger flashed across our bond. Pure, undiluted rage. But Nero didn't speak. I wasn't sure that he could. Something had taken him over.

"An angel's mark can be removed, albeit with great difficulty," Damiel said. "But a bond like yours—a bond forged in love, not only possession—is a whole other kind of magic altogether. It is one of the most powerful kinds of magic there is. And it is for life."

Nero punched through the support beams holding up a carnival stand. Wood splinters shot in every direction, and toy unicorns poured down to the ground.

"Only death can remove it," Damiel finished.

And then it all clicked in my head. Nero's pain. His anger. His helplessness. The only way to harness the power of our bond, to feed it into the Magitech generator and save millions of lives, was for me to die.

7

ANCIENT MAGIC

I swallowed hard and looked at Damiel. "You knew this was coming. You knew this was the test."

"Yes."

Hot, angry tears burned in my eyes. I didn't try to pretend I wasn't scared; that would have been a lie. I didn't want to die.

Wood and metal crashed. Nero had punched through another stall.

"This scenario has been playing out for hundreds of years," Damiel continued. "The City of Ashes cannot be saved. It's not meant to be saved. The gods rigged the trials to test Nero, to see if he would give up that which he holds most dear in order to save humanity."

I'd thought I knew the gods were ruthless and cruel, but I'd never truly known it until now.

"Don't think you can just do nothing," said Damiel. "The gods are fully prepared to watch the Earth's cities fall and humanity die. If the angels didn't know they were willing to make that sacrifice, then this test wouldn't work."

The gods wanted Nero to prove how far he would go—

how much he would sacrifice—to do his duty and protect the Earth.

"I refuse to sacrifice Leda for the sake of a game." Nero looked like he wanted to demolish the whole carnival, but he folded his quivering arms together and turned to his father. "There must be another way, another source of magic to power the generator."

"You can't kill yourself instead, if that's what you're thinking," replied Damiel. "If you did, the gods would kill her anyway."

"I know." Nero wrapped his arms around me, holding me to him. It was a silent promise to me that he wasn't going to let me die.

I didn't want to die. I still had so much to do, so much to live for. I had to find my brother. And Nero… I knew there was more for us. This could not be it. For it all to end like this now, in the gods' game, it would be like my life had meant nothing.

But my life didn't mean nothing to the First Angel. Nyx wanted me to be an angel, and I couldn't become an angel if I were dead. She'd known what she was sending us into. There had to be a way out of this. There was always a way out. If only I could see it.

"You found a way out in your trials, right?" I asked Damiel. "Cadence was the person most dear to you, and she didn't die."

"The test was designed to give you no way out," Damiel told me. "Even I did not find a way around that. I had to sacrifice my best friend, using our bond of friendship to save the city."

"This city? You saved this city?"

"Yes."

"I don't understand. If you saved the city, why is it lost again?"

Anger burned in Damiel's eyes, those eyes that were usually under complete control. "Because the city isn't meant to be saved," he growled. "Once the test is over, the gods throw it back to the wilds so they can use it again to torment the next unsuspecting angel."

My mouth dropped in outrage.

"My trials took place when Cadence was pregnant with Nero. She was about to give birth to the first child of two angels, so she was considered too important to risk her life on missions. She couldn't be my second for the Gods' Trials. That alone saved her life." Damiel clenched his fists. "If my trials had happened at a different time, any other time, she would have died—and for *nothing*." He hissed the word.

"I've always wondered why you turned away from the Legion, even long before they marked you for death," Nero said. "This was the reason, wasn't it?"

Damiel laughed. The sound that came out of his mouth was neither joyous nor jolly; it wasn't even human. It was a sound born in the deepest, darkest part of his soul.

"Yes, the Gods' Trials were the beginning of my fall from grace," he said. "When I sacrificed my best friend in the City of Ashes, I thought I was saving the world. But it was just another one of the gods' games. It was all for nothing, a meaningless sacrifice."

"Is there another way?" Nero asked his father, his eyes pleading, desperate. I'd never seen him look at Damiel that way.

"I knew you would one day face this same choice. Hate me all you want, Nero. I deserve it. I was a cruel father. A hard father. But I do love you. And after I lost my best friend,

I swore I would never see my son forced to make the same choice. There is another way. It took me centuries to find it. There's a magic source hidden in the city, one powerful enough to restart the Magitech generator and save everyone."

"The gods brought it here?" Nero's brows drew together, as though he couldn't believe the gods would offer us an easy way out.

Neither did I. The gods wouldn't give us a magic source that solved all of our problems. This test wasn't about magic. It was about an angel doing whatever was necessary to fulfill his duty to protect the Earth.

"No, not the gods," Damiel said.

"You?" I guessed.

"Leda, I'm flattered, but even I do not have enough power to wield the magic it requires to bring it here. It is an ancient artifact, one that precedes the gods' time on Earth. The cruel immortal minds who designed these trials don't even know it's here. It is made from the same kind of magic as your bond."

"Ancient magic," Nero said. "A cheat."

"This whole test is a cheat. It's rigged. You're supposed to lose, no matter what you do. Sacrifice the one you love to save humanity, or sacrifice humanity to save the one you love. But find this artifact, and you can use it to save the world. And to save Leda from the cruel fate the gods have made for her. Unless you are afraid," Damiel challenged him.

Nero met his father's stare. Respect shone in his eyes. Respect and understanding. Nero understood what happened to Damiel, how the gods had pushed his father away, how Damiel's need to protect him had governed his actions for two hundred years.

"Thank you." Nero extended his hand.

Damiel shook it. But when he tried to step back, Nero's grip tightened, holding him there.

"I still don't completely trust you," he told his father.

Damiel laughed. "I wouldn't respect you if you did."

And then, just like that, Damiel disappeared. The fog rolled in, swallowing the carnival of my memories. A white light flashed before my eyes. When my vision cleared, we were back in the power building, standing right where we'd been before the trance. Well, one of us was standing anyway. My hands and knees were pressed to the ground, surrounded by dust bunnies and brick bunnies. And glass bunnies. At least none of them had come to life while we were out.

Nero reached down and locked his arm with mine, pulling me up. I was barely standing on my own feet again when Nero shook and tumbled. I caught him before he hit the floor. He'd lost another power.

"We will get through this. You'll get your magic back," I told him, stroking my hands down his face.

He steadied himself. "I would withstand the agony of losing my magic a million times over before I ever let you go, Leda."

"Nero…" My voice shook. Joy and pain twisted up inside of me. That was the most romantic thing anyone had ever said to me.

"We need to scour the city for this ancient magic source," he said, his mouth hard with determination.

"Something tells me that we don't have to go far."

He looked over my shoulder to see the big 'x' I'd apparently scratched in the sand while kneeling on the ground. I'd also drawn an assortment of symbols around it.

"I guess I wrote that during the trance." I showed him my dirty fingernails.

"What does the text mean?"

"X marks the spot."

"X marks the spot?"

"Yeah, that," I said. "It's the way to the ancient artifact. And I think the symbols are instructions on how to get there."

Nero's eyes panned across the symbols. "I've seen these markings before. They belong to one of the ancient languages, one not of this world. I can't read them. Can you?"

"I think so."

"How?"

"I don't really know," I admitted. "I guess the same way I have weird visions of things that happened long ago."

"Can you translate them?"

"I can try." I read the first line of symbols. "You need the blood of a black flower." I frowned. "The blood of a black flower?"

"A black rose. When you shred the petals, they bleed."

He opened one of the pouches on his belt and grabbed a handful of black petals. Then he drew his knife and shred the petals to pieces. The moment they hit the x, a black liquid oozed out of them.

"Five drops of blood from an angel," I said.

Nero slashed the blade across his hand and squeezed his blood onto the 'bleeding' rose petals. The growing pool of black liquid flashed, turning the color of caramel.

"Next is—"

A crash of metal cut through my words like tempered steel. I turned to face the latest menace to crash our party. The silver…thing was a few inches taller than me, modeled in the shape of a man.

"What is that? Monster or machine?" I asked Nero.

"Both. The wild magic out here infuses life into metal, forming it into machine monsters."

I looked across the machine man's hard chest. Every line was defined, even exaggerated. Any bodybuilder would have killed for that body. "He has nice muscles." I smirked at Nero.

He returned my stare, clearly not amused.

"Hey, I was just kidding. You are much sexier than he is." I set my hand over his as he moved to draw his sword. "You perform the spell to access the artifact." I drew my own sword. "I'll take care of the monster."

"But you don't have any magic," he reminded me as I ran toward the silver machine.

"I was kicking ass long before I had magic," I called back. "And I was doing it in style. You worry about breaking that seal. I'll keep the monster busy."

Mr. Muscles swung a punch at me. I ducked and darted around its shiny silver body, and his fist slammed through the wall like a wrecking ball, taking a huge chunk out of it. Tiny slivers of shattered brick pelleted my face.

"The next ingredient is vampire blood," I called out to Nero. "Hey, I'm starting to sense a pattern here."

Nero took out a small vial and poured the vampire blood over the seal. It gurgled and popped, swirling into the other ingredients. The mixture was a real boiling brew now. Flames licked the surface.

I darted around a stone column to avoid Mr. Muscles. The machine smashed right through it like it wasn't even there. Broken stones crashed down on me, slamming me to the ground. Coughing out dust and blood, I pulled myself up again and swung my sword at the machine. The blade bounced off his chest.

Mr. Muscles looked down at the scratch I'd etched into his metal abs. His eyes pulsed with crimson fury. He swung his arm, hurling me across the room, and I smashed into a supply cabinet. It tipped over. Tools and cables spilled out all around me.

"Are you sure you don't require assistance?" Nero asked me.

Mr. Muscles stood in front of a brick wall a few feet away, stomping on the tools that had fallen out of the cabinet. He might have had the body of a man, but he had the mind of a child.

"I'm fine. Keep the fire going." I got to my feet, picking up an axe that had spilled out of the cabinet.

"What is the next ingredient?"

I charged at the machine. He swung a punch at me. I ducked and turned. He pivoted with me and punched again. His fist smashed through the wall of bricks behind me. He'd hit it with so much force that his fist got stuck inside the wall. Grinning at him, I swung my axe. The blade cut through the soft material at his elbow, severing the lower part of his arm. The chunk of metal fell at my feet.

I kicked the silver arm toward Nero. "The next ingredient is silver. The more, the better."

Nero grabbed the arm and tossed it into the bubbling mixture. The silver melted, turning the liquid white.

Mr. Muscles came at me again, knocking the axe out of my hand. I grabbed a hammer and a handful of nails off the floor. The machine was armored, but there were weak spots. And though he was made of metal, he shared some similarities to a human body. I rolled and hammered a nail into the Achilles tendon on his right leg. The monster dropped to its knee. I hammered at the same spot on his other leg. He collapsed to the other knee. I picked up my axe again and hacked off the monster's remaining limbs at the joints. Silver machine parts broke off in all directions, tumbling into Nero's potion.

He looked at the mangled machine parts sinking into the white liquid, then at the axe in my hand. "You sure have an interesting style," he declared.

I tossed the axe aside. "I aim to please."

The influx of silver had ignited the potion. Pillars of white flames bubbled and burst out of it. There was a snap and crunch, like the breaking of an enormous tree branch. The ground collapsed under us, and we tumbled into a chasm.

8

MAGIC AND STEAM

*N*ero and I fell through the floor, sand and severed machine parts raining down with us. I landed hard on my butt. I squinted, trying to penetrate the darkness, but my now-human senses weren't up to the task. The air was thick with dust. I couldn't see it, but I could feel it. It was hard to breathe down here.

Then, suddenly, lights glowed to life all around me, illuminating the darkness. We'd fallen into a grand chamber. The floors were marble—pale white, like a sheet of ice. Runes were scattered across the icy marble surface, painted in glittering, shimmering strokes of gold pixie dust. The walls were covered in gold and green emeralds. Light shone from within the walls, basking the room in sparkling light. It looked like a king's treasure room.

Glass display counters kissed the room's perimeter, filled with more treasures than I'd seen in all my life. I rose to my feet, my bones creaking in pitiful protest. When this was all over, I was taking a long, hot soak in a bubblebath. I'd never felt more human than right now. Getting my ass kicked was even less fun when I was mortal.

I'd gotten so used to depending on my magic. The Legion was my life now. I was not human. Not anymore. Standing here now, feeling weak and helpless, I realized that I could never go back to being human again.

"You told me once that I was always meant to join the Legion, that my path would lead me to it," I said to Nero.

"Yes. It is who you are."

I squeezed his hand. "I think… I think despite everything that has happened, until now there was still a part of me that never truly believed it."

"But you do now?"

"These changes, gaining these powers—this isn't about becoming something else. It's about becoming who I am. I didn't realize it back then, but I'd never really felt whole until I joined the Legion. It was as though something were missing from my life."

"As though a part of you were missing."

I nodded.

"I felt the same before gaining my powers. It is a common sentiment amongst the children of angels," he told me.

"But I am not a Legion brat. I didn't have even the slightest hint of magic before joining the Legion, not like the children of angels do. I was completely ordinary."

He chuckled. "You might not have had magic, but you are far from ordinary, Leda. There is magic in your soul, shining through."

"What am I?"

"I do not know."

"I need to know. I know it won't change anything. I am what I am. But I just have to know."

He set his hand over my heart. "We'll figure it out. Together." His voice was both fierce and gentle.

"Together." No other word in all the worlds held so much power. I closed my hand over his.

Then we turned to face the display cases full of trinkets and treasures.

"What is this place?" I asked. "A treasury of some sort?"

Nero scanned the contents of the cases. "A magical treasury of powerful artifacts. All of them have names." He pointed at a pure white bow. "Surefire. It is said that an arrow shot from this bow never misses."

I moved on to the next case, which held a cloak that shimmered like a pot of liquid gold. Its magic was fluid, shifting with the light. "What about that one?"

"The Invincibility Cloak," he said. "When you wear it, weapons go right through you without hurting you." He indicated the next treasure, a pair of leather boxing gloves. "They're called Meteor Shower. A strike from them is said to feel like a barrage of meteors." His eyes dipped to the shelf below, where a necklace of a hundred diamonds lay.

"I've heard of that one," I said. "Divine Tears. It heals any injuries or sicknesses, no matter how dire, of the person wearing it. I thought it was just a myth."

"These are the stuff of myths and legends, lost long ago, but they are very real," replied Nero. "They are all the work of the immortal magic smith, Sunfire."

"These were made by the greatest magic crafter of all time?"

"Yes. These are powerful items," said Nero. "Some of the most powerful in all the worlds."

"So this is the gods' treasure trove?"

"No. If the gods knew about this place, they'd have taken the treasures far away, not left them here for the angels they sent on their trials to find. These artifacts are too powerful. The gods crave power above all else. They could not resist using these objects of power. This is a treasure trove of the original immortals, the powerful beings who preceded gods and demons."

"The Guardians," I whispered.

He gave me a strange look. "You broke the seal to this room. You read the symbols. Their language."

"I told you, I don't know how I did it." The sparkle of the immortal artifacts drew my gaze. "There is magic in these treasures."

"Yes, powerful magic. But there's no way for us to channel that magic to restart the Magitech generator. We could not break these artifacts, even if we wanted to. They are indestructible."

"If we could channel the magic from them…" I sighed.

If only we had Lightning Spear, the lightning rod of magic kept at Storm Castle. It was one of the immortal weapons made by Sunfire. It had the power to absorb magic. We could have used it to channel the magic of these artifacts into the Magitech generator.

But we didn't have the Lightning Spear. And, as Nero had pointed out, we couldn't break these immortal artifacts either. Why had Damiel told us the answer was here? What did he think we could do with the artifacts?

And then it hit me. Damiel had been there when I'd controlled the weapons of heaven and hell, which were also immortal artifacts. He thought I could control these too, that I could direct their magic into the generator. I stared at the display cases full of immortal artifacts, willing them to obey my commands.

Nothing happened.

"It's not working." I turned to Nero. "I can't control them."

"It's not your fault. You don't have any magic right now."

"No, it isn't just Ronan's potion. That magic, whatever it is, is different. It just won't come to me again. I wasn't able to control the weapons of heaven and hell after our return from the Lost City either." I sighed. "Either Damiel overestimated my abilities, or there must be something else down here that can help us." I looked past the display cases, to a large door at the back. "What about that?"

Made from the same pattern of gold and emeralds, the door was wide enough to drive a car through. It was exactly the kind of door that led to a walk-in vault.

"A treasury within a treasury? Whatever is behind it must be very powerful. Maybe we can use it to infuse magic into the generator."

I walked up to the door and brushed my hand across the surface.

"It's hot," I said. "Like there's a fire raging on the other side. I wonder if there's something powerful inside.

Nero touched the wall, tracing his fingers across the rippled surface. "The answer isn't what's beyond the door. It's the seal itself. There is more magic in this seal than even the First Angel can wield." He pointed out the glowing symbols that had appeared on the door in response to my touch. "I have an idea. Don't go anywhere."

He took a running start and jumped up through the hole in the ceiling. I hoped there weren't any more monsters up there.

Glowing runes continued to pop up across the door. They looked familiar, not quite the same as the symbols I'd drawn upstairs, but close.

"What are you hiding?" I whispered to the door.

It whispered back, speaking in a language I didn't know. I leaned in, trying to make it out. What was it saying?

"Leda."

I jumped back in surprise at Nero's voice. "Oh, hi." My heart still racing, I looked at the thick cable in his hands. "What is that?" My eyes followed the path of the cable up through the hole, where it disappeared into the darkness.

"We don't need the Lightning Spear," he told me. "We're going to channel the magic directly into the Magitech generator.

"How?"

"A powerful spell sealed this door, the likes of which I've felt only once before."

"In the Lost City on the Black Plains," I remembered.

"Yes. In the Lost City, you broke the seal to the vault that held the weapons and armor of heaven and hell. Break this seal, and we'll use its magic to restart the city's Magitech generator."

"I'm not even sure how I broke the other seal."

"You can do this. I know you can."

I took a deep breath and set my hands on the door once more. The seal's magic simmered beneath the surface. It was singing to me. I brushed my hands across the door, trying to find the way in. The gold and emeralds melted into a smooth, shiny surface. The runes shuffled around, burning brighter.

Metal crashed behind us. I stole a glance over my shoulder. Three large machines stood under the hole in the ceiling. They shared as much in common with Mr. Muscles as a lion shared with a truck. They looked less humanlike, more cobbled together.

"I think the monster machines are drawn to the generator," I said. "To this place of tainted magic and corrupted technology."

"I'll handle them. You worry about breaking that seal," Nero told me.

69

I leaned my head against the glowing door. I saw a city of magic and steam, its buildings towering high into the sky. Airships, dozens of them, flew overhead. And down below, trains shot in and out of the city. The doors to the train station opened, and people streamed out onto the city streets. I followed them to the power building. Except back then—whenever *then* was—it hadn't held a Magitech generator. Sunlight streamed through a stained glass ceiling that depicted winged warriors.

I took the glass elevator down to the basement, to the treasure room. A magic smith stood in front of the vault door. I couldn't make out his face, like it was cloaked behind a thick haze. Magic flowed around him, shaping the metal. Bands of golden light intertwined with the gold and emeralds, melting into them.

The magic smith touched his hand to one of the glowing runes, the symbol that represented wings. He moved the wings rune across the door's metal face. The door clicked, and a golden knob slid out.

A growl of rage and pain jolted me out of the vision. One of the machine monsters was in pieces, but two still remained. And Nero lay on the floor between them.

I grabbed my axe off the ground and smashed it through the display cases. I reached inside and grabbed the boxing gloves, hurling them at the machines. Then I tossed the necklace at them. I threw each and every immortal artifact in that room. Mesmerized by their magic, the machines jumped and dove to get to them. They forgot all about Nero. I ran to him, helping him up.

"More are coming," he said, snatching a glowing hammer off the floor, one of the immortal artifacts. He slammed it into a machine monster. It shattered like a broken mirror. "Get that vault open."

I ran back to the vault door, scanning the glowing wall of runes for the wings. I found them, way up at the top. Of course they were. I hopped up. It took me three tries, but I finally caught the symbol on my finger and slid it lower. It clicked into place. I grabbed the golden knob that had appeared, turning it.

The door emitted a loud pop, followed by the creak of turning gears. The seal broke, and a white light flashed across the door, shooting down the magic cable Nero had connected to it. It glowed like a rainbow of liquid glitter.

Upstairs, the Magitech generator revved up again. Magic exploded, shattering the glass roof—and every window in the building. Through the broken windows, I saw the golden lights sparkle across the city wall. As the Magitech barrier rolled up around the City of Ashes, a magic shockwave shot through the streets, obliterating every monster inside its borders.

Its seal broken, its magic spent, the vault door groaned. The runes flickered out. The door swung open, and treasure spilled out like a raging river. Gems, gold, jewelry, weapons, armor—the river of treasures knocked me and Nero over, carrying us across the room.

As we collapsed onto the mountain of treasure piling up under the hole in the ceiling, I felt the gods' potion strike its final blow.

"Are you ok?" I asked, taking his hand.

"Why wouldn't I be?"

"You've lost your magic."

He caressed my cheek, his touch soft, his face free of pain. "But I didn't lose you."

"See? I told you we could do it," I said. "We make a great team."

"Yes. We do." His voice was serious, laden with things

71

---

unspoken. He dipped his mouth to mine, his kiss slow and sensual. "Leda."

"Less talking, more kissing," I said against his mouth. My hands curled around the back of his neck, drawing him in closer. I'd never been happier to be alive.

He captured my hands, pinning my wrists to the mound of treasure. "Leda, this isn't the time for this…"

"Coward," I taunted. I arched beneath his steel grip, my breasts straining against my torn tank top.

His gaze dipped to my chest. "You fight dirty."

I smirked at him. "Always."

His mouth came down hard on mine. His kiss was rough, possessive. Desperate. Like I'd just returned from the dead, and he wasn't ever letting go of me again. That was fine by me.

Magic flashed, engulfing us in white light. When the air cleared, we weren't in the treasure room anymore. Nero, the mountain of treasure, and I had been transported into an open chamber even more grandiose.

Climbing roses curled up the tall, white columns that reached into the endless sky. Every thorn, every petal, every leaf was exactly where it should be—as though a master artist had painted the scene. The chamber had no ceiling, no walls. Blue skies and fluffy wisps of clouds lay beyond the columns.

Nero pushed himself off of me, then we stood, sliding a little as we descended the pile of gold, gems, and immortal artifacts. In front of us, seven steps led up to a platform where seven gorgeous people sat on seven gorgeous thrones. Their bodies glowed with ethereal light. I was staring into the faces of the gods.

Ronan, Lord of the Legion, looked down on us from his throne and declared, "Welcome to heaven."

9

THE COUNCIL OF GODS

I looked up at the seven gods sitting on their seven thrones. This was the Council of Gods, the gods who ruled over the Earth. Nero knelt before them, and I followed his lead.

"Rise," said the goddess who sat on the center throne.

She had to be Valora, I thought as we rose to our feet. Valora, the Queen Goddess, leader of the gods' council and ruler of heaven. She looked exactly as I'd always imagined a goddess would look: tall and slender with long, golden curls that fell across her face and cascaded down her back. Her dress was white silk with gold stitching and tiny diamond beads. The skirt was made of airy chiffon that flowed and floated in the breeze.

Her fingernails were perfectly shaped. They were colored just the right shade of pink to look natural, yet more perfect than nature could ever create. It was like she'd been born with a manicure. She wore light golden slippers with beaded pearls. A gold drop necklace with a single diamond accented her dress's low neckline, and her tiara made her hair sparkle.

Gold and white, diamonds and pearls—that was the Queen Goddess.

"Nero Windstriker has completed the trials. The gods will now pass judgment." Valora looked at Ronan, who sat to her immediate right. "What says the God of Earth's Army?"

Earth's Army. That was another name for the Legion of Angels.

Ronan's throne wasn't made of crystals or gems. It was made of beautifully-crafted dark metal. It had the mark of a weapon smith, not a jeweler. Such smooth and perfect lines —such balance, such fierce beauty. Soft light reflected off his throne, making it appear almost liquid. Like a molten river of metals flowing in perfect harmony, in constant, fluid motion.

Ronan was not dressed in the battle leather he'd worn the last time we'd met, but instead in a tunic and pants made of midnight silk. His clothes were still cut very much like a suit made for battle. He certainly stood out next to Valora in her soft, flowing lines and delicate chiffons.

"Nero Windstriker demonstrated uncommon skill and reclaimed the City of Ashes in record time and without any casualties," said Ronan. "There is no question that he should be promoted."

I turned at the sound of a harsh, dissenting grunt. It had come from a god dressed in a very similar Battlefield-in-the-Ballroom outfit, also made of dark silk. His hair was even darker, nearly black.

Valora turned her head toward him. "Faris, do you have something to say, or did you just swallow a fly?"

I'd never met the gods before, but I did know their names. Everyone on Earth knew their names. Faris was the God of Heaven's Army; his soldiers were all gods. They fought in battles against demons and other unearthly beings.

I'd heard there were many such armies, at least one on every world the gods ruled.

Faris looked at Ronan. "You've gone soft, Ronan. Is this you speaking or your half-breed lover?"

Ronan's face was as hard as granite, void of emotion. He looked at Faris with total and complete indifference. "Colonel Windstriker's performance warrants a promotion. The Legion needs more and stronger angels. You have only your own failures to blame, Faris. If your army hadn't lost against the demons at the battle of—"

Valora held up her hands. "We will discuss this later, gentlemen. The topic of this session is Colonel Windstriker's trials."

"Let's discuss that." Faris's hard eyes turned on Nero. "Tell us, Colonel Windstriker, what was the purpose of the trials in the City of Ashes?"

"To restore the magic barrier around the city and reclaim it from the plains of monsters," Nero replied in a crisp and practiced soldier's voice.

"But the mission turned out to be more problematic, didn't it?" said a goddess dressed in a beautiful outfit that reminded me of the witches' attire.

She wore a brown corset crisscrossed with gold ribbons— and tall leather boots under a skirt that was short in the front and feathered out to a train in the back. Her dark hair was twisted up onto her head, styled in an ornate design decorated with gems and feathers. This must have been Meda, the Goddess of Technology.

"Yes, the city's Magitech generator was corrupted with weak, decaying magic that was slowly spilling across the continent's greater grid," Nero told her. "That contamination would eventually bring down the entire system. The barriers would fall, and monsters would flood into every city in

North America. There was no way to disconnect the tainted generator from the grid. Our only option was to push so much magic into it that it burned the contaminated magic away. Which is what we did. The monsters were purged from the City of Ashes, and the corrupted magic in the generator was destroyed."

"And how did you fix the Magitech generator without your magic, Colonel?" asked a goddess who looked exactly like Meda.

If it hadn't been for their different dresses, I wouldn't have been able to tell them apart. Meda's twin wore a long, blue gown accented with strips of gems. A long cape poured off her shoulders like a waterfall. Like Meda, who wore a belt of tools at her waist, this goddess had a belt full of potions and medical instruments. She was obviously Maya, the Goddess of Healing and Meda's twin sister.

"We channeled the magic from a seal that locked a treasure vault hidden beneath the city," Nero told her.

Maya nodded. "Very clever."

"No."

The word echoed off the columns, magnified by magic. It was spoken by a god dressed in long robes. His robes bore some resemblance to the clothing worn by the Pilgrims, the preachers of the faith, often referred to as the voice of the gods. This god's robes were not plain and humble, however; they shimmered green and blue, as though gemstones had been crushed into the fabric. His sandals were gold, his hair paler than mine, and his nose proud. Zarion, the God of Faith, Lord of the Pilgrims.

"The trials were designed to test an angel's commitment to protect the Earth," he told Nero with a disapproving sneer. "Your willingness to sacrifice that which you love most for the greater good." His haughty gaze shifted from Nero to the other gods. "Colonel Windstriker cheated."

"It was an act of brilliance and creativity. Something you wouldn't appreciate, Zarion." Meda's full lips broke into a smirk that was almost human.

Zarion ignored her. "Colonel Windstriker is not an idiot. He knew very well the purpose of these trials and what we were really testing. True, he may have saved the city. He may have followed the letter of the law, but not the spirit." Zarion pounded his fist against the palm of his other hand. "It was an act of defiance. Of blasphemy."

Maya rolled her eyes. "Calm down, Zarion. No one is spitting on your holy pages this time."

Meda snickered.

"I must agree with Zarion," the seventh god finally spoke.

He wore robes too, but his weren't shimmery or ostentatious. They were quite plain actually. It was what he wore over the robes that made them extraordinary. Flowering vines crisscrossed his chest, twisting around his shoulders and down his arms. A dozen Monarch butterflies sat on his shoulders, slowly pumping their wings. This was none other than Aleris, the God of Nature. He spoke to flora and fauna alike. He even whispered to the weather.

"Life and death are a part of life, even immortal life," Aleris said. "Colonel Windstriker found a cheat, a way to avoid the natural order of things. This test was about his willingness to do what it takes to protect the Earth. But he didn't make a choice. He got everything: his lover and the world."

"Yes. That's exactly it." Zarion nodded. "To borrow a human expression, he wanted to have his cake and eat it too."

Ok, that was it. I could listen to this nonsense no longer. I stepped forward. "I wouldn't borrow expressions from the misguided naysayers of humanity. Of course Nero wanted his cake and to eat it too. If I get a cake, what am I going to do with it? Put it in a glass case up on a pedestal and throw it longing looks throughout the day? No, if I get a cake, I'm damned well going to eat it. There is a purpose for cake in the universe, and that's for it to be eaten. There's nothing more natural than that."

Zarion gave his hand a dismissive wave. "You were not given permission to speak, girl. Especially not to speak such nonsense."

The God of Faith might have been irked by my words, but Maya and Meda sure looked amused. Ronan remained perfectly stoic; I wondered if he had any other expression. I didn't look at Nero. I didn't have to. I could feel his stare burning through the back of my head.

But I was too upset to stop now. I turned to Aleris. His frown was more reflective than angry. Maybe I could win him over.

"This whole test is a cheat," I said. "It's a setup. It's as unnatural as things get. Those monsters aren't natural. They don't belong in a human city. So when Nero 'cheated', he was just besting you at your own rules. And, let's be honest, that's what's really got your back up. He won at a game that was designed to make him lose no matter what he did."

Zarion looked ready to smite me—or do whatever it was that angry gods did. But Valora spoke first.

"Nyx was right," the Queen Goddess said to Ronan. "She is lively." She met my eyes for a brief moment, then addressed the other gods. "Now we shall vote." There was a note of power in her voice, leaving no room for disagreement. "Should Colonel Windstriker be promoted for success or executed for failure?"

Dread sank like a stone in my stomach. I hadn't realize

that was the other side of the Gods' Trials. I should have known, though. With the gods, it was all extremes. Reward or death. I wondered if I'd even helped at all by speaking out.

Valora looked at Ronan.

"Promote," he replied. "Colonel Windstriker has been a valuable angel. Without him, the Legion will be weaker, less equipped to fight the darkness that lingers at the horizon."

"Promote," said Meda. "I was impressed by his ingenuity."

"And by his compassion," Maya agreed. "As well as his ability to surprise us. He and Leda are a powerful and resourceful team, even without their magic."

I had the feeling that the two sisters often saw eye-to-eye. Three votes yes. I almost dared feel hopeful.

"You have given me something to think about," Aleris told me. "But it will require much reflection. I cannot vote to promote at this time, though I do not believe Colonel Windstriker should be executed either. I must abstain."

"Execute for blasphemy," Zarion declared.

What a shock.

Valora spoke next. "As explosive as Zarion is, I cannot argue that he has a point. As Queen, I must uphold the laws, both as they are written and the spirit of them. And you failed the test we gave you, Colonel Windstriker. I must vote for execution."

Vicious delight danced across Zarion's face.

Now I was starting to get worried. Three for Nero. One abstained. Two against. Faris was the last one to vote, and he didn't seem to be a fan of Nero—or of Ronan either. So when he voted against Nero, what would happen? Would Aleris be forced to vote in order to break the tie? He was obviously someone who didn't change his opinion quickly, so if he had to vote, he'd go against us.

Valora looked at the God of Heaven's Army. "Faris?"

Faris rose from his throne. He looked fully prepared to take a victory lap over Nero's grave. "It's no secret that I don't approve of the way Ronan runs his Legion. He allows the angels far too much leeway. He doesn't have them fully in check, and as a result, he has lost many of them to the demons. Colonel Windstriker is just the latest example of an angel out of control, breaking the rules, defying us."

He was going to condemn Nero to death. I just knew it. I steeled myself for a fight. A fight against the gods. This was completely insane. Against seven gods, Nero and I didn't have a chance, not without our magic. Hell, we wouldn't even have a chance *with* our magic.

"However…"

The room echoed with that single word. My fists relaxed slightly. I held my breath.

"There is much more to take into account," Faris continued. "Colonel Windstriker and Leda Pierce have saved this world countless times. As much as their methods annoy me, I cannot deny that they are effective. The Earth would be less safe without their watchful, tenacious eyes. It would be a gross oversight on my part to rob humanity of some of its best defenders. Furthermore, the treasury of ancient immortal artifacts they uncovered will greatly enrich my army's powers. So I see no other option but to promote."

Zarion jumped to his feet and shouted, "You are only voting that way to spite me! Like you always do."

Faris's smile was as cold as winter's breath. "Not *only* to spite you, Brother. I gave several other reasons."

Magic flared up around Zarion, a gold and crimson halo of fury. It burned so bright, so blinding, that I had to shield my eyes.

"Enough," Valora's voice cut through his halo like a hot

knife. "The votes have been cast. The Council has voted to promote Nero Windstriker."

Zarion's halo faded. A clear chalice with a gold handle materialized in Valora's hands. I recognized the drink inside, that liquid silver. It was pure Nectar, the food of the gods. I'd seen it once before—when Harker had tried to get me to drink it shortly after I'd joined the Legion. Drinking this Nectar would make Nero an archangel, the highest level of angel. It was as close to a god as any of us ever would be. *If* he survived. At the declaration that we would not be executed, my racing pulse had calmed, but it spiked again now.

Ronan took the chalice from Valora. He walked down the seven steps to us, handing the chalice of pure Nectar to Nero. He turned to me. A second chalice appeared in his hand. The Nectar inside glistened like a sunset.

"For your part in recovering the lost immortal treasures, for your part in the birth of a new archangel, Leda Pierce, I, Ronan, the God of War, Lord of the Legion of Angels, am promoting you to the fifth level." He handed me the chalice of sunset Nectar. "We are intrigued with you—and look forward to see what you will do in the future."

Ronan ascended the steps and took his seat. All the gods were sitting on their thrones now, looking down on us. I had to admit it was unnerving. I'd thought I would have more time to train, to prepare for this. What if I wasn't ready?

Nero set his hand on my arm, turning me toward him. "You are ready." He didn't need magic to know what I was thinking. I guess it was all out there on my face—my uncertainty, my fear.

I put on a brave smile. "As ready as I'll ever be, I guess." I lifted my chalice. "Cheers."

We clinked glasses, then I emptied the Nectar in one go.

That was the only way to do it—quickly, before I had a chance to panic. The Nectar slid down my throat, as smooth as honey.

A surge of heat flashed through my body like wildfire, pushing out the cold that had suppressed my magic. It ignited my powers one by one, skill by skill. I felt my magic returning to me, filling that emptiness inside of me. Like a rollercoaster rolling faster and faster, magic exploded inside of me, and my knees gave out.

Nero caught me. His hands burned against the naked skin on my shoulders. "Steady."

My eyes panned up the ripped and rugged contours of his chest. My fingers followed, snagging on a slash in his jacket.

"We need to heal you," I said, feeling dizzy.

"I'm fine now."

I peeled back the fabric and, sure enough, his skin was perfectly smooth. Any cuts he'd once had were gone now. My gaze lifted, meeting eyes that burned with green fire.

There was a flash of magic, and then we were somewhere else. Somewhere dark. I blinked, my supernatural senses slowly returning to me.

We were back in New York, I realized. I recognized the alleyway, even at this late hour. I'd once cornered a pair of rogue vampires here. We were only a block away from the Legion's New York office. The gods had sent us back here, just like that.

"How do you feel?" I asked Nero.

"Alive." His fingers stroked down my arms.

Goosebumps prickled up on my skin, responding to his soft caress. "It was hard for you without your magic."

"That was nothing compared to the fear that I'd lose you. Down in the city. Then up in the gods' court."

"You looked ready for a fight," I commented.

"So did you."

"No one is taking my angel from me. Not even the gods." I almost choked on my next words. "I will fight to the end for you, Nero."

He wrapped his arms around me, pulling me in. "I can't believe I almost lost you."

"I can't believe I almost lost you." I breathed in a deep sigh of relief.

His scent ignited my sleeping senses. So dark. So masculine. I dipped my face to his neck, drinking him in. It was the most intoxicating scent I'd ever smelled.

I kissed him softly. His pulse pounded beneath my lips, stronger than ever before, pumping with magic. The magic of an archangel. I had to taste him, to feel his blood and magic inside of me. Every pop of his pulse ignited a fresh throb of searing, excruciating need.

"Do it." His voice was a deep rumble in his chest.

"You've just been through so much." I drew away.

His hand locked around the back of my neck, holding me there. "Do it. I want you to feel the magic I'm feeling."

My fangs burned in my mouth, throbbing with such raw hunger that my entire body quivered. His heartbeat thrummed in my ears like a racehorse. I could hear nothing else but that sweet siren's melody. It consumed me. Filled me.

I grabbed him roughly and sank my fangs into his neck. His blood flooded into my mouth, pure and sweet. It burned through my body like liquid ecstasy, its fire searing my flesh, inciting my desire. I couldn't bear the thought of the mere inches between us, let alone thousands of miles.

"Neither can I," he said. "I want you with me. Always."

Had I spoken aloud, or was he reading my thoughts? I

couldn't think straight enough to care about how needy I sounded. I *did* need him.

His fangs teased my neck, stoking that need.

I made a noise that wasn't even human. "Bite me," I pleaded.

He lifted his mouth from my neck, and I moaned in protest. I clawed at him in wanton desperation, pushing his mouth back to my neck, willing him to bite me.

But he was stronger. He captured both my wrists with a single hand. He traced the fingers of his other hand down my neck, pausing at my collarbone, circling it lightly as a devilish smirk curled his lips.

His hand plunged lower. He ripped off my torn top without ceremony and tossed it aside. Fabric tore, and my bra followed. His mouth cupped over my nipple, sucking hard. Pain and pleasure pierced my body. I thrashed and twisted, pressing myself against the hard wall of his chest as I tilted back my head to expose my throat. I couldn't decide what I wanted more: for him to bite me or to have his sweet, sinful way with me. I only knew with complete certainty that if he didn't hurry up and do one of those two things *now*, I was going to die.

"Nero," I moaned.

He lifted his mouth to my neck, whispering into my ear, "Leda."

"Please." My voice was a desperate whimper.

His teeth teased the throbbing vein in my neck. "I want to hear you say it. Say you're mine."

I was breathing so hard, it couldn't have been healthy. "I'm yours."

"And I am yours," he told me.

His fangs penetrated my throat, his kiss scorching me

deep. Heat spread out from my neck, pulsing through my body.

Nero knelt before me, and with a single, rough tug, he relieved me of my shorts. There was a second flash of movement, and then my panties joined them on the ground. His hands traced my inner thighs, parting my legs.

He looked up at me. Gold and silver sparks swirled inside his eyes, igniting the emerald fire. "I can't wait. I have to have you now."

The night's emotions—the fear, the joy, the triumph, the love—it all mixed together with the Nectar and blood. A whirlwind of blind, dizzying desire crashed through me. I couldn't wait either. I grabbed desperately at his belt, tugging it loose.

A deep, feral growl buzzed on his lips. His hands closed roughly around my hips, bolstering me up as he thrust into me. My back hit a hard metal fence, but it didn't hurt. I couldn't feel anything but him.

My hands locked around Nero, holding him tightly to me. "I am never letting you go."

His hands closed around my wrists, moving harder, faster. Every thrust sent a shockwave of fire spiraling through me, consuming my flesh, my blood, my magic. I gripped Nero's back, desperate moans spilling out of me.

A sweet, spicy aroma flooded my senses, and then his dark wings burst out of his back. Velvet-soft feathers rustled between my fingers where hard, smooth muscle had been just a moment before.

I stroked my hand across the tops of his wings. They were so unbelievably beautiful. So hard, yet so soft. His body responded to my touch, his skin buzzing with raw, barely-contained power. And when I caressed his wings again, that control snapped. He groaned deep in his throat, the power of his release pushing me over the edge in a rush of cascading pleasures.

When I finally pulled myself out of the cloud of ecstasy, I realized he'd torn apart the fence we were leaning against—and that my top lay in tattered pieces on the ground.

I slipped into my shorts, shaking with laughter. "We should probably get changed."

He shrugged off his jacket, sweeping it around me to cover the tears in my shirt. Who said chivalry was dead?

"I have a message from Nyx." His eyes panned across his phone screen. "She has a new mission for me."

"Let me guess," I said as we walked down the street. "Babysitting baby dragons?"

"Close. I'm babysitting a baby angel."

"Baby angel?" I frowned in confusion. "But there are no baby angels…" Oh. "You mean a *new* angel. Harker."

"Yes. Nyx wants me to assess his performance as the new leader of the New York office."

"So that means you'll be around for a while?"

"Yes."

I beamed at him. I just couldn't hold it back, even as we entered the Legion office. "It's a good thing it's so early in the morning."

"Why?"

"So there aren't any witnesses to my sappy smirk. Team Lero has a badass reputation to uphold."

His brows lifted in confusion. "Team Lero?"

"You know, Leda plus Nero. Lero." I winked at him. "It has a nice ring to it, no?"

He said nothing.

I sighed. "No, you're right. It's lame. No need to humor me."

He reached over to squeeze my hand, but dropped it when Ivy came down the stairs.

"Back from the trials so soon? How did it go?" She stopped, her eyes panning up and down my body. "Whoa? What happened to your clothes, Leda?"

"Uh, well…"

Ivy looked from me to Nero, and a knowing smile curled her lips. "Oh, I see. Well, I'm glad the trials were *productive*."

"Very funny," I replied.

Ivy threw me a final smirk, then hurried off down the hallway toward our apartment.

"Mind if I change at your place?" I asked Nero, following him up the stairs. "I'm afraid to be alone with her right now."

"Poison Ivy is harmless."

"You only say that because she's too afraid of you to tease you to your face."

"I take it that means she teases me behind my back."

"A little," I admitted, chuckling.

"And do you?"

"Do I what?" I asked as we entered his apartment.

"Tease me behind my back."

"Oh, no. Teasing you to your face is loads more fun. I sometimes even get an eyebrow twitch out of you."

His brows arched.

"Yeah, just like that," I said with satisfaction.

I dumped my ruined clothes into the trashcan, then grabbed a change of clothes from the spare closet in his bedroom. Nero walked up behind me, his hands closing around my shoulders. As I slipped into a new top, his mouth dipped to my neck and kissed me softly.

I pivoted around to face him. "You are making it really difficult for me to put on my clothes."

"That's because you have it backwards."

I looked down at the shirt I'd just put on. "It's not inside out."

"I didn't say inside out. I said backwards." His hand traced my side. He slid my shirt over my head and tossed it to the floor. Then he tossed me onto the bed.

10

COGS IN THE COSMIC MACHINE

"The gods are more human than I expected. Especially Meda and Maya," I said later as Nero and I walked down to the canteen.

"Don't allow their superficial human behavior to fool you," he replied. "They are far from human. That show they put on around us is just that: a show. They enjoy playing human. Never forget that they are far more dangerous. In fact, the sisters might just be the most dangerous of all the gods on the Council. They are fiercely loyal to each other and vote as one. For now, we amuse them. But if we get on their bad side, you will find them considerably less charming."

"You've dealt with the gods before."

"A few times. The first was in the aftermath of my parents' supposed deaths. The loss of two angels drove the gods to call a hearing into the matter."

The way he said 'hearing' was foreboding.

"It was more like wide-scale torture," he told me. "For immortal beings who live forever, the gods are very impatient. They wanted answers now, and they didn't care how many people had to bleed for them to get those answers."

"Charming."

"The gods might look like us, Leda, but they are not like us. Angels were once human, but the gods never were. They don't see things in the same way."

"They enjoy torturing others to make themselves feel more powerful. To feel above us all."

"Yes," he agreed. "We were fortunate that in addition to being merciless, they are also mercurial. They weren't feeling particularly murderous today. That is why we survived."

"I'm afraid I didn't help. I should have kept my mouth shut."

"Not this time. You…*amused* them. You especially amused the sisters. And Aleris." A tiny, confused crinkle formed between his eyes, as though he still couldn't believed that we'd survived. "I think that's the only reason we are alive. That and Faris's desire to annoy his brother."

"Faris did seem to get a kick out of voting against Zarion."

"Zarion is infamously paranoid. He perceives everything as a slight to him, as an attack on his divine rights. He considers himself highly holy, holier than the other gods. Even holier than Valora. I knew he would speak out against us. I have a feeling the Gods' Trials were designed by him— and that he believes we made a mockery of him."

"And Valora? Why did she vote against us? She seemed sensible."

"She is, but as the head of the gods' council, she must uphold the status quo, the gods' laws," he said. "And the truth of the matter is, we cheated on their test. It doesn't matter to them that the test was unfair. Angels are forged in the fire of their own suffering. The gods want us tormented, apart from others. We fight one another; we hold no bonds stronger than those to the Legion, to our duty. We are equal to none. We are above others, serving as their protectors. Never as their friends."

I touched his arm. "It doesn't have to be that way."

Nero lifted my hand to his lips. "I know. United we are stronger. It is the isolated, inhuman angels that we lose— either to their own sadistic cruelty or to the demons' army."

"I think Ronan realizes that."

Nero nodded. "Yes. Nyx has made him more human. He sees things differently than he used to. He is less rigid, less concerned about the rules, about the semantics of every encounter. He cares more about what's really important. It took losing Nyx for him to see the bigger picture."

I wondered what had happened, but I figured it was not Nero's place to tell Ronan and Nyx's story.

"The rest of the gods do not have that connection to Earth. Not like Ronan," said Nero.

"If the gods don't care about us, why are they here? Why did they come to Earth?"

"They are here watching over us because they need to hold our world against the demons. It is just one part of a much bigger game."

"These other worlds have gods and demons?" I asked.

"The gods hold some worlds, the demons others."

"Just how many worlds are there?"

"A lot," he told me. "We're talking about hundreds of worlds. Maybe thousands. I don't even know. I've never been beyond this one."

So this was just one gigantic, cosmic war between light and dark magic. And we were only a small part of it, a tiny dot in the gods' empire. It was no wonder that they saw us as insignificant.

We entered Demeter, the canteen, to the clink of plates and silverware and the hum of conversations. It was early in the morning, at the dawn of breakfast, but the tables were already packed. There wasn't a free seat in the whole room. Except at the head table, where the officers level six and above sat.

"Follow me," Nero said.

As I followed him across the room toward the head table, conversations died all around us. Everyone froze and stared —no gaped. Nero was wearing his new uniform with an archangel pin—wings and crown halo—the symbol of a general. It wasn't every day that an archangel joined us for breakfast. Nero had extended his wings wide. They rustled and shimmered like a cloak of midnight magic.

Harker rose to his feet, the only person in the whole room who'd remembered protocol. The officers at the head table followed suit. Reminded by their example, the rest of the soldiers in the room all stood in respect. Nero and I passed rows and rows of soldiers at attention. I caught Ivy's eye, who winked so quickly that I almost missed it.

I was wearing my new pin too, a paw print, the symbol of Shifter's Shadow. We stopped in front of the head table. I swallowed hard, trying to clear my discomfort. I might have been an officer now, a lieutenant, but the head table was reserved for only captains and above. I didn't belong here.

Harker saluted Nero. "General Windstriker."

"The First Angel has assigned me to evaluate your performance. I will be watching you." Nero's eyes flickered to me. It was a silent signal to Harker that he wasn't only watching Harker for Nyx. He was watching him to protect me too.

Harker nodded, looking resigned. Some of the spark went out of his eyes. He had to know Nero would be hard on him in his evaluation.

As smooth as a summer breeze, Nero circled around the table and took the seat next to Harker. It was the one reserved for the First Angel when she visited New York. He waved me forward, toward the empty chair beside his, the seat usually occupied by Captain Soren Diaz. Soren must have been out on a mission right now. I moved toward the chair, the weight of several hundred pairs of eyes on me.

Sit down, Pandora, Nero spoke in my mind.

I did as he asked. Every other person in the room was still standing, including several Legion officers who held a higher rank than I did. Including an *angel.* They all continued to stand, waiting for Nero's signal. Nero was obviously playing this game for a reason.

Nero raised his hands in the air, then motioned for everyone to sit. All the while, Basanti was watching me from her seat on the other side of Harker, looking positively amused.

I could hear the whispers in the room. The conversations were divided between shock over where I was sitting and excitement over Nero's promotion. A trio of female soldiers at a nearby table stared at him in wonder. From the long, leisurely looks they were casting down the length of his body, I bet they were picturing him naked. I met their eyes with a wide smile and stroked my hand across Nero's.

Mine, I broadcast silently to them.

The women hastily looked away. Nero captured my hand in his. He'd obviously liked my show of outright, territorial force. Such were the ways of the angels.

"You two are creating quite a stir," Harker commented. "Everyone is staring at you."

I smirked at him. "They are just admiring Nero's wings."

Nero's new wings were simply stunning, even more gorgeous than they'd been before. New patterns had formed in the tapestry of black, blue, and green feathers. He'd explained to me earlier that Nectar changed the swirls and patterns in an angel's wings. Great battles and bursts of powerful magic could change them too. They were the story of an angel's magic.

Harker chuckled. "At least some of that attention was for you, *Lieutenant*." His eyes flickered to the pin on my jacket. "I must say that the gods' magic becomes you. You're positively glowing. And I'm not the only one who's noticed."

He glanced at a group of male soldiers who were casting appreciative looks my way. Nero met their eyes with a cold stare, and they all suddenly became very interested in their breakfast plates.

"You can't blame them, Nero," Harker said. "Look at that halo. She is practically lighting up the whole room." His eyes slid over me with appreciation.

"She is mine." Nero's voice was deceptively calm.

Harker met his eyes. "Oh, you've made that abundantly clear. Your mark is screaming at me. You are anything but subtle, Nero."

He'd marked me again upstairs, burning his archangel magic into me. I could still feel it pulsing, absorbing into my blood and magic. When I'd marked him too, he'd given me a very satisfied look and told me that my mark was growing more powerful with my magic.

"Your magic is growing beautifully, Leda," Harker continued. "I look forward to helping you grow it further."

"What?"

"Didn't you hear?" He smiled at me. "I am in charge of training you now."

Nero was very quiet. He was watching Harker like his former best friend was going to pull out a vial of pure Nectar at any moment and force it down my throat.

Don't worry. I can take him, I told Nero.

Do not underestimate him, Leda. He is an angel now. He is much more powerful than before.

I looked at Harker. "Your training me—this is Nyx's orders?"

Harker braided his fingers together, looking very pleased with himself. "This comes straight from the Gods' Court."

It seemed our little meeting in heaven had caused the gods to take an interest in me. That wasn't a good thing. As Nero had reminded me earlier, the gods saw us as little more than cogs in the cosmic machine. Their interest had nothing to do with helping me and everything to do with using me. One of the gods was already interested in using my connection to my brother Zane to hunt him down. That was the god who'd given Harker pure Nectar and instructed him to make me drink it, not caring if I died in the process.

But which of the gods was pulling Harker's strings? Which god was trying to manipulate me to find Zane? Was it the same one who'd tried to poison me with Venom? It could have been one of the gods who'd voted for me and Nero to live so that I could fulfill that purpose.

But then again, the gods were deviously divine. Harker's patron god might have voted against me and Nero because he knew how the votes would fall. Or she. Could it be Valora? She did what was best for the gods, humanity be damned. I could totally see her commanding Harker—and him following her commands. She was the Queen Goddess, after all.

Then again, it could be any one of the seven gods. It could even be a god not on the council.

"You are speechless," Harker said to me.

I wasn't sure how I felt about him training me. We'd once been friends. I wanted to trust Harker, but he'd already betrayed me. And I would be naive to think that he wouldn't do it again. Fundamentally, he was a good person. I knew he was. But his ambition was too strong; it drove his actions. What I really wanted was for Nero to train me. I trusted Nero.

The doors to the canteen swung open with a bang, and a soldier stormed into the canteen, running to the head table. He stopped before Harker and declared, "The ocean is rising fast. It's going to flood the city."

11

MAGIC GONE WILD

*H*arker looked at the soldier. "Who is responsible?"

He asked that because natural weather disasters weren't our job to fix. The elementals handled them. But stopping the supernaturals behind threats to the Earth's people was very much our job.

"A water elemental was spotted at the shore," the soldier reported.

The way he said it made it clear that the water elemental wasn't trying to stop the tidal wave.

"She is waving her arms around," the soldier continued. "She is coaxing it, conducting its movements."

Harker looked at Basanti. "Captain Somerset."

Harker was putting Basanti in charge of the team, a good choice given her powerful elemental magic.

She nodded, standing. "Claudia, Morrows." She pointed them out in the crowd. Her eyes found Drake. "Football." That was his nickname because before joining the Legion, he'd been a star football player. Basanti looked at me. "You too, Pandora. You're almost as good at averting disasters as you are at causing them."

It was a compliment. I think.

We rushed out of the room, running to the garage. Claudia hopped into the driver's seat of a big white truck and immediately revved up the engine and switched on the siren. The garage door slid up, and our truck shot out onto the street. Traffic parted before us. People always made way for the Legion. They knew we were saving lives. Plus, they were afraid of us. People who got in the way of Legion missions were considered as guilty as the criminals we hunted.

In the back seat of the truck, Alec Morrows was sorting through his sizable gun collection. How in the gods' names did he expect to carry all of those?

When he saw me staring, Alec smiled and petted his enormous pitch black block of a gun. It didn't look like a usual weapon, but when you saw it, you knew you were staring your own mortality in the face. "Like what you see, Leda?"

I should have known better than to respond, but I just couldn't help it. "Where did you get that Hellfire?"

The Hellfire was a 20mm RPG that shot magic bullets. Literally. The metal for the bullets had been mixed in the fires of hell, a magic fire hotter than any on Earth. The weapon had powerful dark magic. It wasn't standard Legion issue. Our magic weapons were powered by light magic.

"I took it off a soldier of hell," he told me. "I nabbed it before he got off a single shot, so it's fully loaded."

That meant ten shots.

"What will you do when you run out of magic bullets?" I asked.

Alec's grin grew wider. "Kill another soldier of hell."

He had a very uncomplicated outlook on life. I often wished that I could see the world in such simple terms.

Alec gave the gun a long, affectionate stroke. "She shoots like a demon."

To Alec, all guns were female.

"We could hit the shooting range when we get back. It will be fun." He hit me with a cherubic expression. "I'll even let you shoot my gun."

"Be careful, Alec," Drake warned him.

"With what?"

"When flirting with Leda."

"General Windstriker isn't here," Alec said.

"No, but he has eyes everywhere."

Alec frowned and looked around, as though he'd find Nero hiding in the corner of the truck.

"It's not General Windstriker you need to worry about, Alec," Claudia told him. "It's Leda. If you annoy her, she'll kick your ass, and there's nothing you can do to stop her."

Alec opened his mouth to protest, but then he must have remembered the last time we'd trained together. He was strong and hit like a wrecking ball, but I fought dirty. I grinned at him.

Alec's frown deepened. "Point taken."

As he went back to caressing his guns, Drake winked at me. He and Alec were the muscle on the team. Claudia was the muscle too, but her magic was pretty damn strong—as I'd learned back on the airship.

Our truck screeched to a stop on the sidewalk. We all hopped out and stared down the enormous tidal wave that loomed over the shore. It was so high that I couldn't see the sun. I couldn't see much of the city or the sky either. That glimmering, glistening wave blocked it all out.

A woman dressed in a blue dress and sandals stood before

the wall of water, her hands raised in the air, her dark hair fluttering wildly around her. The elemental was clearly still growing the wave. As soon as she let go of it, it would crash over the city.

Basanti stepped forward. "I command you to stop in the name of the Legion."

The elemental turned around to face us. Her blue eyes pulsed with magic. She waved her hand in an arc over her head, the swirls and bubbles of water responding to every flick of her fingers. Little droplets of water hung in the air, moving in slow motion around her. Her hair swirled in that same slow-motion stream. She looked like the personification of magic gone wild.

Basanti barked out another warning, but the elemental didn't seem to realize we were here. It was like she was in her own world. Her eyes flashed again. They were nearly white now.

"See if you can talk her down, Pandora," Basanti said.

"Me? I'm not a negotiator."

"You have powerful siren magic."

I stepped forward, my hands open, empty of weapons. I reached for the elemental's mind—and hit a wall of pain, desperation, and fear. I tried to break through that wall, to influence her. "I can feel that you're in pain. You don't want to hurt anyone."

"Help me." Her voice cracked with agony.

"We're going to help you," I promised her. "But you have to stop the tsunami, or a lot of people will die."

"They're everywhere!" the water elemental shouted. Her eyes flickered wildly from one spot to the next. "I have to drown them!"

I kept moving toward her. "Who? Who is everywhere?"

"The monsters."

"We're with the Legion of Angels," I said soothingly. "We will take care of the monsters, but you need to stop this wave before it destroys the city."

Fear flashed in her eyes. "It's too late. The monsters are here, lurking in the shadows. They've already taken over. There is nothing you can do."

"Where are the monsters?"

"Everywhere." Her hands shook. "There is no escape."

A wall went up in her mind, ejecting me. My magic snapped around me, and I stumbled back.

"What happened?" Claudia asked me.

"I can't influence her. She pushed me out. I have a feeling she's battling for control of her own mind."

"Demon possession?" Drake asked.

I shook my head. "No, it's something else. I don't know what it is that's made her like this. Fear perhaps. Whatever these monsters she saw were, they have her absolutely terrified."

I closed my eyes and concentrated, but no matter how hard I pushed, I couldn't get back into her mind. I was cut off. I couldn't influence her.

"The monsters won't matter if she destroys the city. She is a threat." Basanti waved us forward. "Take her down. Stop that tsunami."

"She doesn't want to hurt anyone," I protested.

"Her intentions are irrelevant. If we don't stop her, she will hurt a whole lot of people."

Drake and Alec tackled the elemental. They slammed into her so hard that it would have knocked out most supernaturals, especially elementals, who had notoriously low physical resistance. But she didn't pass out. She stumbled to the side, recovering quickly. Her arm swung out like a propeller, knocking them aside. Drake and Alec flew past us and slammed into the truck. No elemental should have had the strength to toss aside two of the Legion's biggest, toughest soldiers like they were nothing more than paper dolls.

She pivoted, waving her hands around. The tidal wave mimicked her movements, crashing forward. Basanti blasted it with her magic. The wave stopped falling, but it didn't dissipate. Surprise crossed Basanti's face for a moment before she buried it beneath the rock-hard facade of her determination.

This was weird. Basanti had powerful elemental magic, so powerful that the First Angel had once offered to make her one of the Dragons, the Legion's keepers of elemental magic at Storm Castle. But despite her exceptional elemental magic, she wasn't able to wrestle control over the tidal wave from a water elemental? The world's supernatural beings could best us in numbers, but one-on-one, a soldier of Basanti's level beat them every time. What was happening here shouldn't have been possible.

Drake and Alec were on the move again. They charged at the elemental. She didn't let them get close this time. Her arm cut through the air. A whip made of pure lightning magic sizzled to life in her hand. She snapped at Drake and Alec, pushing them back.

This was even more bizarre. Some very skilled water elementals could also cast ice magic, but no water elemental could summon lightning—or any of the other elements for that matter.

This water elemental had not only demonstrated power over another element; she had demonstrated the strength and resilience of a vampire, which was another kind of supernatural altogether. The only people who had the abilities of multiple supernaturals were soldiers of the Legion. Or soldiers in the Dark Force of Hell.

Drake and Alec attacked her again, one from each side this time. The water elemental caught Drake in a whirlwind, then scooped up Alec. She thrust out her hands, and the wind funnel hurled them both into the ocean. The water bubbled up, churning around them, pulling them under.

I ran past Basanti, who was still battling the tidal wave, her brows scrunched up in concentration. She couldn't hold off the elemental's magic for long.

I reached for control of the whirlpool dragging the guys under, but its magic snapped me back. The water elemental had repelled my spell—and she hadn't been gentle about it.

"Fine, be that way," I growled at her and jumped into the water.

Alec had enough elemental resistance to push against the magic tide and breathe underwater for a few minutes, but Drake wasn't at that magic level yet. I locked one arm around him and swam for the surface, resisting the magical turbulence. As I dragged Drake to the shore, Alec surfaced. He grabbed onto Drake's other arm and helped me cut through the spell that was trying to pull us in deeper.

We stumbled out of the water, falling onto the lumpy shore. A whip of water burst out of the ocean and snapped at us. I jumped up and blasted a ball of fire at it. The tentacle dissolved—then quickly reformed. I blasted that one apart too. One after the other after the other, the tentacles kept coming.

A gunshot went off. I turned to look. Claudia had shot the elemental in the leg. The elemental didn't even blink. It was like she was so lost now to the madness that she didn't even feel it.

Through my battle with the water tentacles, I saw Claudia shoot her a few more times. None of her bullets appeared to have any effect. She couldn't even knock out the elemental.

Basanti dropped to her knees. She was losing her battle with the tidal wave. It swelled again, pushing toward the city.

Claudia threw down her gun and drew her sword. She ran at the elemental, swinging her blade. The steel sang in the air, sparkling with magic fire. She slashed through the head with her burning blade. The elemental dropped to the ground, dead.

In an instant, the magic dissipated. The tidal wave receded, the water spilling back into the ocean. We all looked from the blood dripping off Claudia's sword to the dead elemental lying on the ground.

Harker was not going to be happy.

12

AFTERMATH

*C*rowds of curious people flocked to the shore in the aftermath of the magic tsunami that nearly drowned New York. To keep them away from the crime scene, Alec and Drake had set up heavy barriers that no mortal could lift. That didn't stop the spectators from eagerly clicking photos as Claudia carried the water elemental's headless body into the truck. I didn't want to think about what that said about human nature.

Drake and Alec stood at the barrier, their thick, muscular arms folded across their chests. Between that and their black vests, leather pants, and thick boots, they looked perfectly terrifying. The crowds were keeping their distance from the barrier. The guys' assortment of swords, knives, and guns was just the cherry on top of the badass package.

They were keeping the paranormal police out too, much to the chagrin of one of the police detectives. He was currently engaged in a heated debate about jurisdiction with Basanti. He shouldn't have wasted his breath. He'd lost the battle before it had even begun. The Legion's authority always trumped any other organization on Earth.

Ivy drove up on her motorcycle, dressed in a leather bodysuit. Heads turned as she took off her helmet and shook out her long red hair in the sunlight. It was like a scene straight out of a shampoo commercial.

She hopped over the barrier and beelined straight for me. "Wow, this looks bad."

"It looked worse a few minutes ago with a thousand-foot tsunami towering over the city," I told her.

"I'll bet." Ivy's eyes panned across the dozens of water puddles that dotted the shore, tiny souvenirs left over from the wave.

"Did Nerissa send you?"

"Yes."

Dr. Nerissa Harding was the leading scientist at the Legion's New York office. She was also my friend. Ivy was one of her assistants.

"Nerissa thought I would be useful if you ran into any more crazed supernaturals trying to destroy the city," she told me.

Ivy was good at talking people down from strong emotions. And she could do it without using any magic. She was just a natural.

"Nerissa really thinks there's more of them?" I asked.

"There's one thing I've learned in my time at the Legion, Leda: there's no such thing as an isolated incident."

I sighed. "I fear you're right."

"The other reason Nerissa sent me in her stead is because she needed someone to check out the scene of the crime. She said she'd had quite enough excitement at Storm Castle and had no desire for any more fieldwork." Her lips curled up. "Especially not with you around because you are a magnet for trouble."

I didn't bother being offended because it was completely

true. I might as well have been going around wearing a t-shirt that read: *apocalypses, psychopaths, and chaos welcome here*.

Ivy set her hand on my shoulder. "It's not your fault that craziness erupts all around you. You're just unlucky."

Drake passed by, carrying another heavy barrier. I could barely have carried that metal monstrosity with both hands. He was using only one. Ivy met his eyes, then they both quickly looked away.

"What was that all about?" I asked.

"What was what about?"

"Nothing. Never mind."

Ivy was really good at reading others, but she was as blind as a newborn kitten when it came to herself—and how madly in love she was with Drake. He was obviously in love with her too. Lately, they'd been stealing a lot of clandestine looks at each other. When Drake and his former girlfriend Lucy had gone their separate ways, I'd thought he and Ivy would finally get together, but neither one made a move. They'd been best friends since birth, so it must have been awkward. I was guessing there was a big, fat boulder of denial standing in their way.

Ivy watched her best friend as he planted the barrier in front of a pair of teenagers who'd tried to sneak past him and Alec. Alec saw Ivy looking their way and winked at her. He must have thought she was staring at him.

Reporters and photographers now stood amongst the growing crowd behind the barriers. Word had spread fast that the city was nearly destroyed. Claudia joined Drake and Alec to play bouncer. The paranormal police detective was still badgering Basanti. He was lucky she was so good-natured. Colonel Fireswift would have long since thrown him at the Legion's Interrogators, the nightmares of the supernatural world.

"Why are we being kept off the battle site like civilians?" the detective demanded.

Basanti pointed out. "You *are* civilians, Detective."

He frowned. I remembered that scowl well. He was the same detective I'd met last year, a few months after joining the Legion. I'd gone with Nero and a few others to the Brick Palace, the site of an attack that was coined the New York Massacre. The detective seemed less impressed with Basanti than he'd been with Nero. Well, when it came to sheer intimidation, it was hard to compete with an angel, especially one like Nero.

"Captain Somerset, I must protest—"

She gave him a flat look, cutting him off. "We're done here. File your protest through the proper channels. I'm sure the Legion's Interrogators would be happy to speak with you."

The detective paled.

Basanti was really channeling her inner angel right now, that part all Legion soldiers had inside of us to some degree. The detective took an uneasy step back. Basanti was definitely changing, growing closer to becoming an angel. The recent events at Storm Castle might have had something to do with her change—that and her reunion with her angel lover.

"I wonder if I could have done that too, channeled my inner angel so well?" I commented.

"I think so," replied Ivy. "You've been practicing your Nero Windstriker face in front of the mirror."

"Oh, saw that, did you?"

"Drake and I both did."

They were my roommates. I wondered if me living with them was holding back their relationship.

Ivy and I turned our attention to the scene of the battle. We scoured for clues, looking for anything that might explain how a water elemental had gained powers she shouldn't have and tried to unleash them on the city. I'd already looked and found nothing but ocean debris and a few tiny sea creatures, but maybe we'd have more luck together.

"So how is Nerissa holding up after Storm Castle?" I asked.

Colonel Fireswift, the sadistic angel who'd temporarily commanded the New York office, had sent her there for hardcore training to punish her. He hadn't liked the way she'd tried to protect soldiers from being forced into his promotion ceremonies, ceremonies he'd used to level up the best and to cull the weakest links.

"She's been well. Thanks to Soren, I think." Ivy smiled.

Soren was Ivy's ex, but they were still friends. Ivy was on great terms with all of her ex-boyfriends. I didn't know how she did it.

"Being with him is good for Nerissa," Ivy said.

"And for the rest of us. As long as she's happy, she has less time to gossip about others."

"Speaking of gossip…"

I cut her off before she could grill me on my and Nero's tattered appearance this morning. "You're next, you know."

Her gaze flickered to Drake. I didn't even think she knew she was doing it.

"There's always another one, Leda. The trick is finding the *right* one. The one who can handle the real me. Someone I don't have to dress up for."

The memory of our last movie night flashed through my

head—Ivy, Drake, and I wearing pajamas and fluffy bunny slippers.

Ivy stopped. "I'm sure it's right in front of my face."

Just as I thought my friend had finally recognized her love for Drake, I realized she wasn't looking at him anymore. Her eyes swept the crime scene.

"But I don't see anything out of the ordinary." She shook her head. "No runes, no glyphs, no strange machines, no potion bottles. Nothing. What caused the water elemental to lose her mind? There's nothing here that would explain her behavior."

"She mentioned monsters. She said they're here."

"Here in New York? I haven't seen any fur, scales, or claws. Or any other signs of monsters, for that matter."

I shrugged. "Maybe she meant demons. Could she have been possessed by a demon?"

"Demon possession leaves a mark on the host's body. The water elemental had no unusual marks anywhere. Besides the missing head." She cringed. "And all the bullet holes. What happened?"

"That was all Claudia," I told her.

Alec was pretty upset he hadn't gotten to use his Hellfire. The gun had been pulled into the ocean when the elemental made it swallow him and Drake. He'd later retrieved it from the water.

"I counted eight bullet wounds in the elemental's body," Ivy said. "Three in the chest. Those wounds should have killed her, but it took decapitation to do that?"

"Yes. Her magic was unlike any elemental's, unlike anything I've ever seen. She wasn't just powerful. She used powers outside the elemental spectrum. That's why I wondered about demons."

Ivy shook her head. "It's not possible. She has no mark.

The gods have put a spell on the Earth so that any demon who tried to possess humans here would leave a mark on their victims."

I knew I was grasping at straws. I knew that the elemental's magic was light magic, not dark magic. Not demon magic. I could feel it when the water tried to pull me under. Light magic vibrated differently than dark magic. So if this wasn't the work of demons, then what was going on here?

"The best we can do is bring the elemental to Nerissa and see if she can find the cause of her odd powers," Ivy said. "Whatever happened with the elemental, it didn't start here. And it won't end here either."

UPON OUR RETURN TO THE LEGION OFFICE, WE GAVE Nerissa the elemental's body to analyze. She was happily doing that now. She really was in her element in a lab, not in the field. I hoped Harker let her stay there instead of antagonizing and pushing her like Colonel Fireswift had. Keeping Nerissa in the lab wasn't just best for her; it was best for the Legion too.

After our detour to Nerissa's lab, we'd headed straight for Harker's office. We were standing before him now, dripping water all over his beautiful cherrywood floor. His eyes took in our soggy appearance, his mouth a hard, thin line. I didn't think he cared about the water as much as the report we'd just given him.

After what seemed like a century of silence, he finally spoke. "The Legion of Angels is charged with upholding the gods' laws and protecting the Earth." He paced in front of us. "When supernaturals attack at the scale that water elemental did today, there's usually something bigger going on behind the scenes. That is why we capture and interrogate rogue supernaturals." He paused before Claudia. "But because you killed the water elemental, we cannot figure out what caused her outburst."

Nero stood beside Harker's desk, watching us all without the slightest hint of emotion on his face. This was his role as observer.

"You should have handled this better," Harker told us.

"At least we saved the city," I pointed out. "And no one on the team died. Nor did any innocent bystanders. Given the situation, that's much better than things could have gone."

Harker was looking at me like I'd completely lost my mind. "That isn't how the Legion of Angels functions."

I was tempted to remind him that he'd once killed a crazy supernatural too, but I held my tongue. He'd killed her out of mercy, so his heart had been in the right place, even though the Legion hadn't liked it. I didn't want to punish him for that small act of kindness.

Basanti stepped forward. "I take full responsibility for Lieutenant Vance's actions."

"You're not going to get her off the hook, Basanti," Harker replied.

"I realize that, but as team leader, her actions are also my responsibility."

They were all crazy. Claudia had done the right thing, and it had saved us all. But clearly Harker didn't see it that way.

"Both of you are off this assignment. In fact, I'm pulling you off all combat missions," Harker told Basanti and Claudia. He swiped his finger across his phone screen. "I'm assigning you two to babysit our latest batch of initiates.

They are waiting for you in Hall Two. Go." He waved toward the door.

It was a punishment, but not a big one. As far as Legion punishments went, it was the mildest I had ever seen. This whole thing was still completely ridiculous. They hadn't done anything wrong.

With Basanti and Claudia gone, the full force of Harker's stare turned on me, Drake, and Alec. "Pandora, I'm putting you in charge of the mission. Don't screw it up."

"Me?" I gasped.

That was a surprise. Why had he picked me instead of bringing in someone new, someone higher up in the Legion?

"Yes, you," he said impatiently. "You are an officer of the Legion now. It's about time you learned how to lead a mission instead of running off by yourself like a rogue, doing whatever you feel like."

I opened my mouth to protest that I never did such things, but I closed it again immediately. He was right. I'd done exactly that many times over.

"Figure out why that water elemental went crazy," he told me. "Take Poison Ivy with you. You need some brains to complement all the muscle you have on your team."

I wasn't sure how to take that. Was he calling me the muscle too?

"Don't just stand there and gape at me, Pandora," he barked. "Get this sorted out. Now."

13

LOVE AND MAGIC

*A*fter that spectacular meeting with the Legion's newest angel, we all headed back to our apartments to change into something less soggy—Alec to his apartment, Drake and I to ours. Ivy was waiting for us in our living room.

"How did it go with Harker?" she asked.

"Pretty much how I expected it to go," I told her. "He was miffed that we didn't bring in the water elemental alive, so he took Claudia and Basanti off the mission."

Drake smiled. "And he put Leda in charge." He patted me on the back.

Ivy nodded slowly. "Interesting. I didn't expect that."

"Thanks for the vote of confidence."

"Oh, you know what I mean, Leda. You're just so new." Ivy gave me a reassuring smile. "But you'll do great."

I smirked at her. "That would have sounded more convincing if you weren't crossing your fingers behind your back."

She lifted her hands in the air, wiggling out her fingers. "I did no such thing."

"I know. I was just messing with you."

Ivy gave me a long, assessing look. "You're nervous."

"Of course I'm nervous. I've never been in charge of people before."

"Sure you have. Back on the Black Plains after the vampires took Nero, you took charge," she pointed out.

"That doesn't count. I told them to stay in town and watch our prisoners while I went off on an unsanctioned solo trek across the Black Plains to rescue Nero."

"It wasn't unsanctioned. Nero left you in charge. And you saved his life."

"Then why did his gratitude hurt so much?" I winced at the reminder of those hundreds of laps around the track and all the extra training Nero had assigned me as punishment.

"He's an angel," Ivy said. "I think their gratitude always hurts."

Drake peeled off his soggy jacket. Ivy's eyes widened.

"What is that?" she gasped.

His brows drew together. "My firm and muscled physique?"

"No, not that." She pointed at the enormous bloodstain on the front of his shirt. "*That*. What did you do to yourself?"

"It's fine."

"Fine?" she hissed. "No, it's not fine. You're bleeding through your shirt!"

"It's nothing. I hardly feel it. The one in my leg is much worse."

Ivy's nostrils flared in anger. "How many wounds do you have?"

He shrugged. "I don't know. A few."

"You need to see a doctor."

"Honestly, I'm fine."

"You keep saying that word, but I don't think you know what it means."

"Ivy—"

"Refusing to take care of your wounds doesn't make you tough. It makes you stupid." She looked at me for support. "Tell him he's being an idiot."

"After you change, you should head over to the medical ward to get the holes in your body plugged," I told Drake. "Then we'll head out."

Ivy glared at me. "He can't go on a mission in this condition."

I looked at Drake. "Are you feeling dizzy?"

"No."

"Feverish?"

"No."

"Shivery?"

He smiled back. "No."

"They're just surface wounds," I told Ivy.

The Legion wasn't a warm and cushy place. We'd all had much worse injuries in training, but Ivy couldn't see that right now. Her emotions were running too hot. How could anyone be so much in love with another person and not even realize it?

"Don't worry. The doctors can heal him in a few seconds." A sly smile curled my lips. "Or you could just let him drink your blood."

Ivy scowled at me. "I don't think either of you are taking this seriously."

Drake snorted, and more blood permeated his shirt.

"Ok, that's it!" Ivy pushed him toward the door. "To the medical ward. Now."

He bowed his head and tried to look contrite.

"Meet me in the garage when you're done," I told them.

He shot me a silly smile. "Yes, sir."

"If you salute me, heaven help me, I will refill all your favorite liquor bottles with cleaning alcohol while you're gone," I warned him.

He chuckled as Ivy pulled him by the hand into the hall. Chuckling a little myself, I went into my room to change.

Nero was waiting for me inside. I didn't jump in surprise —this time—but my heart sure did.

"How did you get in here?"

Nero gave me an amused look. Right, stupid question. He'd been lord of this cosmopolitan castle for years. He knew his way around and could bypass any lock. He'd left Harker's office after us, so I was amazed he'd beaten me back here. Then again, he had his mysterious ways of getting around.

"Why are you here?" I asked, my pulse finally slowing.

A slight smile touched his lips. "Does my presence agitate you?"

The look in his eyes was smoldering. A rush of heat flushed me, right down to my pinky toe, and my pulse sped back up. I was agitated all right, but not in that way. I tried to keep calm, even knowing it was futile. He could read my body and knew exactly what effect he had on me.

"Agitated?" I repeated, sliding my closet door open. "No, of course not."

I grabbed a fresh change of clothes and a towel to dry myself off. I was still dripping from my unintended swim in the ocean. Nero just stood there, a silent menace. I wondered if he was going to stand there the whole time and watch me strip out of my soggy clothes.

"I've seen every part of you, touched every part, tasted every part."

His words caressed me like a silk pillow kissing naked skin. Images of our passionate predawn tumble in the alley flashed through my head. Blushing, I stopped. I realized that I'd moved toward him, nearly touched him.

With a soft chuckle, he reached out to take my hand. He flipped it over and kissed the underside of my wrist. Then he bowed, his eyes never leaving mine, and proclaimed, "I'll await you in your living room, my lady."

He turned smoothly on his heel and left my bedroom, closing the door behind him. My heart jumped in my chest. I was simultaneously excited and disappointed by his actions.

I stripped quickly, drying myself off using a magic wind dryer. Then I changed into fresh clothes and headed into the living room. Nero was standing before the fireplace, looking over some of Ivy's decorations that were set atop the mantlepiece.

"Your roommate has peculiar taste in tabletop ornaments," he commented, holding up one of them. "I have traveled the Earth, been through heaven and hell, and I've never seen anything like this."

"It's an oversized teacup without a handle," I told him.

"You can't drink tea out of that. It's made of straw," he pointed out.

"It's a metaphorical teacup."

Nero looked at the object in his hand. "Your metaphorical teacup bears an uncanny resemblance to a moon charm."

"A what?"

"A moon charm. It's a kind of love charm." He set it back on the mantlepiece.

I blinked in confusion. "Ivy doesn't need love charms. She has more admirers than anyone on Earth. No, it's a teacup. Or a candy bowl."

Nero's eyes panned across the room. My pulse jumped when I realized that he'd never been inside my apartment before. I really wished it would *stop* doing that.

Nero's gaze shifted to the kitchen counter. "Pandora, you are wicked."

I realized I'd just been fantasizing about throwing him down on that counter and having my way with him. And he'd heard my thoughts. What was wrong with me? My body reacted to him every time he was near, making me think things, want things. It was like I had no control over it whatsoever.

"It's our bond, an effect of me marking you," he told me. "That part of me inside of you draws you to me."

Yeah, like I needed magic for that. I was drawn to him already. My blood hummed like the engine of a high-speed train whenever he was near.

"Will it diminish?" I asked him.

"You'll get used to it."

I didn't fail to notice that he hadn't really answered my question. Well, it was my fault for jumping into a relationship with an angel without asking about the consequences first.

"Are there any other side effects I should know about?" I asked.

"Nothing that should affect you now."

Not now, but later? That was hardly comforting. What other side effects were waiting in my future? I decided I really didn't want to know. I'd cross that bridge when I came to it.

"I marked you too. Why don't you feel the same way about me?" I asked. "Why aren't you out of control? Why aren't you drawn to me?"

He stepped toward me. "I can assure you, I'm very much out of control." His body towered over me, so close I could scarcely breathe. "I shouldn't be alone with you, Leda. Not when we both have places to be. And," he added, leaning in.

119

"I've never been more drawn to you." His voice was seductive, his words kissing my ear.

I reached for him, but he'd already stepped back.

"You look pretty firmly in control," I commented, my heart thrumming in my ears.

His lips parted. "Oh, Leda, how very wrong you are. Right now, I am putting everything I have into blocking out the call of your blood, your body." His gaze slid over me, burning me like a live wire. He took a deep breath and folded his hands together behind his back, as though he couldn't trust them. "Your magic sings to me. And it's only growing. Had you been an angel when you marked me, no amount of willpower would be enough to stop me from taking you now."

I felt myself moving toward him.

"So, you see, you are stronger than you think," he said. "An angel's mark is powerful, especially a new mark. I'm surprised you are holding back."

That might have had something to do with the number of times we'd had sex in the past two days. It was strange to remember how young our bond was. It felt like it was so much older, that it had penetrated deeper into my magic.

"You're wrong," I told him, also folding my hands together behind my back. "I'm not strong."

Somehow, despite our nights of passion, I still wanted him. I needed to get my mind off of this, or we'd never leave this room. I grasped for distractions. He'd come here for a reason—a reason besides having sex with me. I could tell he was here about something else.

"What do you think of what happened in Harker's office?" I asked. His reason for coming must have had something to do with that.

"Harker is under pressure. He's wanted to be an angel for

as long as I've known him, and if this situation blows up now, so close to the beginning, it could compromise his position."

"Nyx has put him under pressure by assigning you to observe and report back on him."

"Yes. It is a common practice when a new angel is made, but there is a reason Nyx chose me to carry out the assessment. And it's not so I could spend time with you. She doesn't quite trust Harker."

"If Nyx doesn't trust him, then why did she make him an angel?"

"She might not have had a say in the matter. If the gods tell her to make someone an angel, she cannot refuse. The role he played in saving Colonel Starborn was an act worthy of becoming an angel. Harker's patron god could have used that triumph to push the other gods to vote for his promotion."

"So I guess that answers our question as to whether Harker still has the support of a god."

"Indeed," he agreed. "And Nyx must realize Harker still has the support of one of the gods. The purpose of my assessment is to see if Harker will be a useful angel in her army, or if he's going to be a problem."

"And what do you think?"

"That it remains to be seen. How he handles these first few weeks will establish what kind of angel he will be. There is a place for all kinds of angels at the Legion."

True. After all, Nyx had managed to fit Colonel Fireswift into her army.

"We angels are not known for our kindness, Leda," Nero said. "Kindness is not something that concerns Nyx. She only cares that her angels will be loyal to her. She doesn't want a repeat of the Legion's early days."

"What happened?"

"A lot of angels went dark and joined the Dark Force of Hell. The exodus was led by an angel very close to her. That betrayal hit her hard. And it's why she is so careful now. She knows not all of her angels are the nicest people, but we are loyal to her and to the Legion. She strikes down any who are not. And she has become even more vigilant now that the demons are trying to make a play into our world."

"Does Nyx know what happened between you and Harker?"

"I don't believe so. If she knew Harker had tried to give you pure Nectar, she would be assessing him herself. She obviously knows something happened, but she hasn't asked me about it. She does know that I no longer completely trust Harker, which is probably why she gave me this assignment. She knows I will watch him for any sign of misstep."

"Harker knows it too," I said. "That's why he was so upset in the meeting just now."

Nero nodded. "This is the first major crisis the city has faced under his command. It did not go well, but crises rarely do. And this one is the perfect problem to test how well he can handle his new position. If Nyx decides Harker will be loyal to her and the Legion, she'll keep him."

He didn't say what would happen if Nyx decided Harker wasn't loyal enough. That was obvious. Nyx had chosen well. Nero would be a fair judge. He didn't want Harker to die because they'd been friends for so long. And he wasn't jumping at the chance to accept him because Harker had betrayed us—well, actually he'd betrayed me, but Nero took that betrayal rather personally.

"How is Harker doing so far?" I couldn't resist asking.

"Nyx would approve of the way he handled the incident. Claudia had to kill the elemental; it was the only way out of that situation. If she hadn't acted, larger parts of the city would have been destroyed and thousands would have died. On the other hand, Claudia's actions robbed the Legion of an opportunity to interrogate the water elemental, to learn how she had acquired her unusual powers."

"Saving the city is more important than questioning her," I declared.

"Perhaps, but what if questioning her could prevent this from happening again?" he posed.

He had a point. Maybe the gods were right after all. Maybe you couldn't have everything.

"Harker punished Claudia for depriving the Legion of answers, and he punished Basanti because she was in charge of the mission," Nero said. "But Harker also demonstrated that he valued and respected them, that he considered them to be outstanding examples of a Legion soldier."

"By putting them in charge of training the initiates," I realized. "That's why he chose that punishment."

"Training our initiates is an important task," Nero said. "The Legion needs soldiers, especially now that the demons are pushing harder to return to Earth. Giving Basanti and Claudia that responsibility is putting a piece of the Legion's future in their hands. You don't put just anyone in control of the survival of our newest soldiers when they are at their weakest. Harker demonstrated that he trusted them with this important task."

"He's always liked them."

"Yes," Nero agreed. "And more than that, he respects them. He handled that well. And he was right to put you in charge of a mission too."

"I was wondering about that. Why me? There are other soldiers, more experienced ones. More capable ones."

"You have proven yourself many times in your short

tenure at the Legion. You *are* experienced and capable. More than that, you don't back down. Harker knows that as well as I do. He saw your magic at Storm Castle. He knows you have the power inside of you. You just need to grow it. This mission is the perfect opportunity for that."

"And growing my magic fits right into his god's plans for me, to level up my magic so they can use me to find Zane," I pointed out.

"That too. Harker is in that way a perfect angel. Everything he does accomplishes many things at once." Nero set his hand on my shoulder. "But that doesn't mean he's wrong to put you in charge of this mission. I would have handled the situation in exactly the same way. You are tenacious and resourceful. You *will* figure this out."

14

THE SEA KING

*L*ater, as my team and I were questioning the city's king of the water-based elementals, I tried to remind myself of Nero's assertion that I was tenacious and resourceful. Right now, stuck in this circular conversation with the Sea King, I wasn't so sure I was the right person for the job.

All of New York's ice and water elementals were under the Sea King's rule, so he should have known everything about them. But he was stonewalling my questions about Serenity, the water elemental who'd almost drowned the city under a tsunami this morning. Such a calm and peaceful name—with a reputation as a calm and peaceful woman—and yet her actions just a few hours ago suggested anything but that.

"What was Serenity's place in your kingdom?" I asked him.

"She was one of our firefighters," replied the Sea King.

Like all supernaturals, water elementals had many key responsibilities, and they all had to report to the Legion at the end of the day. One of those responsibilities was firefighting. It was well-suited to their skills. Just as earth elementals grew food and flowers. And the fire elementals made good blacksmiths.

The Sea King continued, "Serenity was very dedicated to her job and to saving lives."

He had been repeating the same line for the past hour. I didn't doubt it. I'd seen the water elemental firefighters at work in the city. They were a dedicated and brave bunch. I wondered if I'd ever seen Serenity out there too.

I could not show my emotions, and I couldn't afford to take his word for anything. "If she'd dedicated her life to saving others, then why did she try to kill everyone?"

The Sea King shook his head. "I don't know. She didn't have a violent bone in her body."

"She appeared agitated during the incident."

It was a vast understatement to refer to the near total drowning of New York City as merely an 'incident', but since no one but Serenity had died, I couldn't really call it a massacre.

"She was shouting about monsters taking over," I continued. "Do you know anything about that?"

His eyes darted up, then he met my gaze again. "No."

He was hiding something. I could feel it in my bones. I considered compelling him to figure out what it was, but I could sense a slight tug on the periphery of my mind. He was wearing an amulet to block mind control. After a particularly unpleasant encounter with a witch and his talisman, I'd learned to always check for defenses before compelling people. It wasn't fun to have your spell bounce back on you.

Maybe I was just paranoid to suspect the Sea King, but I didn't think so. Why would he wear an amulet like that unless he had something to hide? Those amulets drained your magic when you wore them; that's how they were powered. It would leave him weaker, more vulnerable. Supernatural leaders couldn't afford to be weak or vulnerable. He must have been feeling pretty desperate—desperate to hide something from us.

Maybe he was just hiding something unrelated, something he was afraid the Legion would find out. Most supernaturals had secrets. And supernatural leaders had more secrets than others. That was the cost of ruling. They sometimes did things the Legion wouldn't approve of—not necessarily bad things, but definitely things on the Legion's very long taboo list. I'd once had to track down a vampire king; he'd hidden away a young vampire child who'd mistakenly killed humans. The child was beloved by her house. A young child couldn't control the gift—or the blood lust.

The Legion had eventually found the child. They'd executed her for the safety of humanity. They had killed the vampire king too, as an example to others, but not before interrogating him for several weeks to see what else he was hiding. The answer was a lot. Being a leader required you to break the rules to keep your people safe. To keep everyone safe.

The Legion considered leaders responsible for the actions of their subordinates. That's why Harker had punished Basanti along with Claudia. He was following Legion protocol to the letter.

"If the Legion finds out you've withheld information, there will be consequences," I told the Sea King.

He sighed. "I understand."

Yeah, he was hiding something. But I wasn't ready to send in the Interrogators just yet. First of all, I didn't have any evidence. And secondly, the Interrogators freaked the hell out of me. I'd once watched them manipulate a witch, the heir to a powerful New York coven, into joining the Legion.

Into giving up everything she had in order to salvage her coven's honor.

"The water elementals have to pay for the damages," I said. "Unless you can point me to the person behind Serenity's outburst."

It was the standard Legion threat. I had been on enough missions like these to have memorized the usual threats we used to get supernaturals to talk.

The Sea King sighed again. "Send me the bill."

So much for taking the lifeline I'd thrown him. I wasn't surprised. I wouldn't have taken the deal either. But I still had to go through the motions, playing out this scene to its conclusion.

"Very well."

I pressed my hands against his desk, leaning in. He might have been wearing an amulet that blocked my siren magic, but I did manage to mesmerize him on a mundane level. He met my eyes, captivated. Maybe it was all the leather I was wearing. The Legion uniform was functional. It was designed to intimidate. And there was nothing like a whole lot of black leather that broadcast intimidation.

"But if I find out you've been impeding a Legion investigation, I won't be pleased." I made my voice very hard.

He dipped his chin in acknowledgment.

I turned away from his desk, looking at my team. "Let's go."

Then I led them from the Sea King's fortress. On the way out, we passed aquarium windows and shimmering orange walls. The place had been fashioned to resemble an underwater castle. It looked like it was made of coral, but the builders had actually used steel and glass—along with a bit of cosmetic magic to make it look like coral.

As we walked toward our truck parked just outside the gates, I asked my team, "How did I do?"

"You channeled your inner angel well," Ivy told me.

"I'm glad you liked it."

"Your tone, your presence. It was perfect. That was the sexiest thing I've ever seen." The look on Alec's face was almost adoring. "Will you marry me?"

I snorted.

Drake patted me on the back. "You were very menacing. Very Legion."

We all climbed into the truck. Drake shut the door behind us.

I typed a few things on my phone, then tucked it into my pocket. "Well, what I'm going to do next is decidedly very not-Legion." I handed them all earpieces and pressed a button on my watch.

Sounds came in, a soft hiss in my ears. The signal cleared, and the Sea King's voice buzzed over the line.

"We have a problem," he said, obviously speaking to one of his people. "We need to deal with it before the other elementals find out—or worse yet, the Legion. Tell Holden to come to me."

Whoever Holden was. I assumed he was another elemental, one of the Sea King's minions. Maybe the one he called when he had secrets that required burying.

I heard the click of the light switch and the whisper of a closing door. And then silence. Everyone must have left the room. I took off my headphones.

"When did you bug the Sea King's office?" Alec asked me.

"When you were leaning forward against his desk, drawing his eyes to you. All of our eyes," Ivy realized.

"Yes. If he knows something, I am going to find out." I looked at Alec. "Let's go."

He climbed into the driver's seat. "Just let me say that I approve of your actions," he declared as the truck peeled away from the curb.

Drake looked at the headphones in his hands. "What is the range on that bug?"

"It's the latest tech. It will cover the whole city. And it's recording to my watch, so I can listen in later." I tapped my watch.

"This is not Legion tech," Ivy commented.

"The Legion has similar tech, but, no, I bought this in the city. It's black market stuff made by renegade witches."

Some girls bought purses and shoes. I bought black market spy gadgetry.

"You need Harker's approval to bug the house of a supernatural leader," Drake pointed out.

Technically, that was true, but I knew Harker wouldn't go along with this. And I had to do what I had to do to save lives, even if it meant being a little renegade. That's what being a leader was all about. It was the same conundrum the supernatural leaders often faced: follow the rules or keep their people safe. Their choices often got them into trouble. And my choice might get me into trouble too. But if someone had found a way to give supernaturals the powers of Legion soldiers, everyone was in danger.

Who was it? It wasn't demons feeding them Venom. Serenity's powers were definitely made of light magic. And Ivy had found no evidence of a demon mark on Serenity's body. Did some god get bored and decide to play games by giving random people Nectar?

"Harker isn't secure in his position," I said to Drake. "He'll want to play this by the books so early on in his angel career. Bugging a leader isn't by the books. The Legion keeps power by fear and force. They also keep it by working with the supernatural community's leaders, and they can't just bug them at random." I took a deep breath, feeling the weight of my decision. "We can't afford to play that game. There's something bigger going on here, as we heard from the Sea King's conversation."

"You're right, Leda," Alec said.

Ivy nodded.

"Ok," Drake said. It seemed Ivy's agreement had tipped him over the edge. "I suppose sometimes unconventional methods are required. We will keep your secret."

"Good, then I don't have to kill you." Grinning, I took back their headphones.

"She's kidding, right?" Alec asked the others.

Ivy just smiled at him.

"The Legion's Interrogators would use everything they heard against him. They'd use it to threaten, blackmail, and coerce him," I said. "But we're not going to play that game. I won't steal his secrets or expose them. I just want to figure out what happened with Serenity."

"You might not like what you hear from the bug," Drake warned me. "Supernatural houses engage in a lot of cruel activity—cruel, but sanctioned."

"I'll deal with it. I have to. Whatever is going on, it's bigger than just that one incident, and that means it could happen again. We have to stop it before something happens and a lot of people die."

It was getting dark outside now. My first training session with Harker was scheduled for tonight. Was it weird that I was looking forward to it? I guess I was just morbidly curious of how he was going to torture me up to the next level of the Legion ladder.

My phone buzzed. I pulled it out. "I've gotten an alert. There's been another incident."

It seemed Harker would have to wait.

"A vampire has gone wild, exhibiting unusual powers," I read on.

Who said lightning never struck twice?

15

MONSTERS

"Drive north two blocks, then turn right at the edge of the Witches' District," I instructed Alec. We were driving to the source of the vampire attack, our sirens flashing. Traffic parted in front of us, but they weren't moving fast enough for Alec. He swerved the truck onto the sidewalk, speeding past the lines of cars. He was driving like a maniac. Usually, I would have complained, but we were in a hurry right now. If the last attack were any indication, we could be in a lot of trouble. A typical vampire had the potential to cause a massive amount of carnage. If his powers were boosted like Serenity's had been—if he'd acquired magic outside the vampire spectrum—then this could turn into nothing short of a disaster.

We were getting close. I could see the trail of destruction. Buildings had holes in the sides; something hard and heavy had been thrown at them. Cars were overturned everywhere. The warped remains of streets signs lay on the pavement, like they'd been used as baseball bats. A car was impaled on a traffic light. I prayed that we didn't find anything else impaled.

"Park here," I told Alec. "This is the place."

The car had barely stopped moving when we all ran out. It looked like a battle site. Blood was splashed across the buildings. There was a low rumble, the love child of a hiss and a growl. It echoed in the darkness, seeming to come from everywhere. And it was growing louder.

A potent electric charge danced across my skin, causing the hairs on my arms to stick up. A strange, unsettling feeling washed over me. It wasn't exactly dread, though I was feeling a lot of that at the moment. My magic clenched up inside of me, like an iron ball in my stomach, like it had eaten something it didn't agree with.

We moved carefully, weapons out, searching the shadows. A bent streetlamp was buzzing, flickering at erratic intervals. A scream shot down the street. We kicked off into a run, following the sound to its source.

When we reached the end of the street, we found bodies on the ground. Two of them were Legion soldiers. They'd been ripped apart, mutilated. My stomach lurched as I glanced across what remained of their uniforms. Corporal Jenkins and Sergeant Lee. They were the ones who'd called in the report. Just minutes ago, they'd still been alive. If only we'd gotten here faster.

A shaking lump lay beside their bodies. I squinted and saw that lump was actually a woman on the ground. Her skirt was torn, and the strings of her corset had split open. It looked like an enormous beast had scratched her across the stomach. The short sleeves of her blouse hung limply against her arms, soaked in blood. The top might have been white once, but now it was stained crimson.

"A witch," I said.

She was bleeding but still alive. Ivy ran to her and began

to mix up potions using the ingredients she drew from the pouches on her belt.

"What happened here?" I asked the witch as Ivy healed her.

The witch's body shook with fear. "A beast. A horrible beast."

"A vampire?"

"Yes." Her lower lip quivered. "And no."

"What do you mean yes and no?" Alec asked.

"It was big. So big. Especially his fangs," she said. "But he was not beautiful like a vampire. He was…wild. A monster."

"Where did he go?" I asked her.

The witch pointed up, her eyes trembling.

I looked up, squinting to see through the darkness. I caught a hint of movement. I ignited a ball of fire, sending it up there to light up the darkness. A vampire fell down from the shadows. He'd jumped off the roof of a hundred-foot building. His bare feet landed on the cobbled ground with a thump, but the drop hadn't hurt him. He was very resilient, even for a vampire.

His eyes were lit up like rubies. Blood dripped from his fangs and fingernails. His pale hair was stained with it. His clothes, the fashionable clubbing outfit of a vampire going out on the town —a silk shirt, a pair of designer jeans, dress shoes—it was all torn to pieces and stained with blood and rust, the latter presumably from the old street signs and posts he'd thrown around.

When the vampire saw us, his mouth opened wide and he let out a horrible noise. The growl-hiss I'd heard earlier belonged to him. There was something deeply primitive about it, as though there was no rational thought left in him, only instinct. The witch was right. He was truly a beast. His eyes shone with uncontrolled rage.

I waved at Drake and Alec. They tried to move toward him from two sides, to surround him. The vampire pivoted sharply, lightning sizzling down his right arm. An electric whip formed in his hand, snapping and hissing as he lashed out at Drake.

No vampire had elemental magic. This was definitely linked to the earlier incident with Serenity. But what had caused this strange sickness that gave them both powers and drove them mad? What was turning them into monsters?

Monsters. That's what Serenity had meant when she'd said the monsters were taking over. The monsters inside of her, taking over her mind. I glanced at the wild vampire. Those same monsters lived inside of him.

The vampire's whip knocked Drake against the wall. Lightning kissed the brick facade, creating a wide laceration with a black burnt line on either side. He swung again, but Drake was already on his feet.

The vampire turned around and, in a flash of speed, slashed his whip at Alec, who'd tried to sneak up on him. Alec caught the lightning whip around his forearm and tugged. It disintegrated into smoke. The vampire roared in fury.

Alec shot at it with his Hellfire, but the vampire was too fast. It ducked out of the way, and the flaming bullet tore through the building behind him.

Drake and Ivy charged at the vampire, but he shifted shape, turning into Ivy. There were two of her now. One of the Ivys grabbed the other and they tumbled onto the ground, kicking and punching.

Alec aimed his gun again, but then he paused. "Which one is the vampire? I can't tell them apart."

Drake shook his head in frustration. "I don't know."

I looked at the two Ivys. It was a powerful spell, a good copy. Thanks to my recent training in shifting magic, though, I could pick out the subtle differences between them. I spotted the vampire in the shadows, behind the Ivy mask. I ran forward and punched him hard in the jaw. I put a lot of magic behind that punch, enough to break through the illusion. The false Ivy shattered, revealing a feral vampire.

"It's sure great to have my magic back," I commented.

I moved in to knock out the vampire, but he darted out of my path, his nimble grace in complete contradiction to the primitive gleam in his red eyes. He was so fast, faster than any vampire I'd ever fought. Faster than I was. I couldn't get in close enough to land another punch.

And then the vampire just froze, his eyes locked on my pale hair. It had mesmerized him, just like it did all vampires. He shared that trait with his brethren. I took advantage of his distracted state and slammed a punch into his head.

He withstood my hit. Damn. He wasn't only stronger and faster than a standard vampire. He was more resilient too.

He struck back with a psychic blast. It smashed into me with the force of a train, flinging me across the dark alley. My back slammed against a building, bricks spilling down on me. I staggered to my feet, my bones creaking, my head pounding, the world spinning. I lifted my hand to the back of my head, and my fingers came back covered in my own hot blood.

The vampire was closing in on me. I swung again, but he was quicker. He caught my hand, and in a single swift movement, he snapped my wrist. Biting back the pain, I drew my knife with my other hand and stabbed the vampire in the side. He knocked me aside like I was a mosquito. And then he went after my companions. He didn't even remove the knife I'd lodged in his side. It was like he didn't feel it at all.

Alec fired the Hellfire again, and this time he didn't miss. The vampire roared with pain, grabbing the gun out of Alec's hand. He twisted it back on itself, then tossed the warped piece of metal to the ground. Alec glanced down at his mutilated gun, a look of total mortification on his face.

He drew another gun and fired. The mundane bullets tore through the vampire. One of those bullets hit the vampire square in the forehead. The shot should have killed him, but it didn't. It didn't even slow him down. Drake charged the vampire, tackling him. The vampire bucked, throwing him off his back.

I shot the vampire with a fireball. If he noticed, he didn't show it. He continued to beat into my companions. Nothing hurt him. Nothing except the Hellfire bullets, I realized. Bullets that were made of dark magic. Dark magic hurt the vampire.

So I changed the tone of my fire, using my dark magic instead of the light. *That* the vampire noticed. He roared and spun around, charging at me. I created a whip of my own, made of dark fire. Everywhere it touched, it cut into the vampire's skin.

But his wounds healed too fast, sealing right before my eyes. The vampire was too close. He was almost upon me. I continued to slash and burn, but he was closing in. I couldn't hold him off much longer. I just couldn't do damage fast enough. I snapped the whip, curling it around the vampire's neck, pouring more dark magic into the spell. The vampire roared, swinging his arms widely. His fist slammed into me and threw me back.

I pushed myself off the ground, pulling a stake out of my leg. A wooden crate had broken apart when the vampire had thrown me onto it. I limped forward on my good leg, clutching my broken wrist. My companions weren't faring any better. Drake was trying to pull a pole out of Alec's torso. Ivy was trying to protect the witch.

I prepped my dark magic. Flames erupted on my unbroken hand. The vampire stalked forward, looking as good as new. There wasn't a scratch on him.

"You have got to be kidding me," I groaned.

The vampire was almost to me.

A growl shook the buildings, and a werewolf jumped out of the shadows. It looked ready for a fight. I was surrounded, trapped by a vampire on one side and a werewolf on the other. And it wasn't just any werewolf. That werewolf was bigger than any I'd ever seen. It was the emperor of all werewolves. Its lips peeled back, revealing a mouth of sharp teeth.

But the werewolf didn't attack me. It jumped over me, diving at the vampire, tackling it hard. Lightning sizzled on its fur, shocking the vampire. I cringed. The werewolf was infected too.

The vampire and werewolf were so busy fighting each other that they'd forgotten all about the rest of us. At least they weren't friends. If they had been, my team wouldn't have had a prayer of making it out of here alive.

The werewolf knocked the vampire aside, then it went for me. It froze, its eyes locked on my hair, mesmerized. Ok, that was weird. So far, only vampires had ever been mesmerized by my hair.

Speaking of vampires...

The vampire jumped up and attacked the dazzled werewolf. They rolled across the ground, ramming into a building. Bricks fell down and glass shattered.

I rushed over to Alec and Drake and, with my good

hand, grabbed the pole jammed through Alec's torso. I met his eyes. "This won't hurt a bit."

"You lying—"

I pulled out the pole. A roar erupted from his mouth. I quickly poured a healing solution over the wound. It sizzled and steam rose from it.

Alec roared even louder. "That felt like acid! What the hell is the matter with you, woman?!"

"That's Lieutenant Woman to you, and you're welcome. I just healed the gaping hole in your stomach."

"You call that helping?" he growled. "I'd rather bleed to death."

"Not in my truck, you don't." I helped him to his feet, then limped toward the truck. "Drake, help him in. Then get the car started."

Drake was staring at Ivy, who was kneeling beside the witch, trying to keep her alive. The vampire and werewolf were fighting around them. The monsters had already nearly barreled them over twice.

I snapped my fingers in front of Drake's eyes. "Snap out of it, Drake. You get Alec inside and start the truck. I'll get Ivy and the witch."

Drake nodded, his face half-apologetic, half-defiant. I zigzagged around the fighting vampire and werewolf, ignoring the throbbing pain in my leg.

"Grab the witch," I told Ivy. "We're getting out of here."

While the two supernaturals were busy trying to kill each other, Ivy lifted the victim into her arms, and we ran back to the truck. Ivy carried the witch. I ran in front, keeping the path clear, which meant knocking the vampire or werewolf out of the way whenever either one got too close. They were so intent on killing each other, they didn't even seem to notice.

We made it to the truck, and I slammed the door shut, shouting to Drake, "Drive! Now!"

As the truck sped off, tires screeching, I only hoped the vampire and werewolf kept fighting each other long enough for us to get away. As soon as one of them won the battle, the winner would come for my team. And I wasn't sure our truck could outrun them.

16

MAGIC EVOLUTION

*T*he witch's name was Charlotte. She told Ivy and Nerissa that as they wiped the blood off her body and assured her that she was going to be all right.

Harker stormed into Nerissa's office. "Are you or are you not soldiers of the Legion of Angels, the gods' army and upholder of the gods' justice?" he demanded. He looked angry enough to demolish a few city blocks himself.

I stepped between him and my team. "We are."

He spoke in a soft, harsh hiss. "Then why, in the name of everything that is holy, did you run from a werewolf and a vampire?"

"They weren't just any vampire or werewolf," I said patiently. "They were different."

Behind me, Charlotte wept softly, as though she were reliving her nightmare in the alley.

"Different," Harker said flatly, clearly unimpressed.

"Yes, different," I told him. "They were mutated somehow. Like the water elemental this morning, their own powers were heightened. And they possessed the powers of many more supernaturals. They were like no vampire or werewolf I've ever seen before. Nothing hurt them. *Nothing.* Not even when Alec shot them in the head."

"Decapitation?" he asked.

"I tried to decapitate the vampire, and it didn't work. His neck was stronger than my weapon. Even when I poured magic across the blade, I couldn't get it through fast enough. Just a few hours ago, Claudia killed the water elemental with decapitation. That is no longer a viable solution. This condition, or whatever it is, has evolved."

"What do you mean *evolved*?"

"I don't really know because I don't understand it myself," I admitted. "I just have this feeling… See, the elemental didn't have as many powers as the vampire and werewolf just now did. It's like they're gaining more powers as time passes. Even in the fight, they gained more powers as the minutes sped by."

"The vampire couldn't put out my fire, and then he suddenly could. Their magic was growing in front of our eyes."

"And you let two highly dangerous supernaturals, who have managed to steal magic, free in my city?" Harker said coldly.

I frowned at him. "They didn't give us much choice."

"There is always a choice."

"Yeah, the choice was to run, or to stay there and fight and let my team and Charlotte die just like the two poor soldiers who came before us," I snapped. "Is that what you wanted?"

Harker bit his lip. I was pushing him too hard. I was betting on my theory that he needed me alive more than he needed to vent. Actually, his patron god was the one who'd told him to keep me alive, and I was reminding him that I knew all about that.

"You are resourceful," he finally said. "You always find a way to cheat death."

And there he was letting me know that I'd escaped death in Nero's trials. Boy, this verbal sparring match was sure fun.

Or did he know about the trials? Maybe I was just being paranoid. The information surrounding the Gods' Trials was kept confidential, even from angels. *Especially* from angels.

"That's just what I did. I cheated death by not throwing my team into death's jaws," I said. "There was nothing we could have done had we stayed there. Nothing we tried did more than annoy the vampire and werewolf."

"Actually, that's not true," Alec spoke up. "You managed to hurt the vampire with your elemental spells."

"I'd hardly say that *hurt* him. Maybe it stung him. In any case, it wasn't enough. I still couldn't hold him off." I shifted my gaze to Harker. "The vampire and werewolf would have killed us, and then they'd still be free. The only difference is we'd all be dead too."

"Your spells still worked better than anything else we tried," Alec persisted. "The vampire survived a bullet to the head. He didn't even wince. But he hurt when you hit him with your magic. How did you do that?"

Speak a bit louder, why don't you? I wished I were a telepath so I could send Alec a mental message to shut up. I did not need him drawing attention to this. The Legion didn't want soldiers with dark magic and light magic. They believed dark magic belonged in the demon's army. And that you couldn't have both at once; that you could only give up one to have the other.

"I didn't do anything special." I shot Alec a smug smirk. "I just train more than you do."

Alec snorted. "That's the truth. I thought I trained a lot. But, woman, you don't do anything but train, train, train."

"Of course I train. I'm dating an angel. Training is good for my sex life."

Ivy gaped at me. Drake coughed. Harker gave me a guarded, neutral look. Alec, however, looked at me like I was his hero. Nerissa chuckled under her breath.

I decided a change of subject was in order. "How is your patient?" I asked Nerissa.

"She's traumatized, of course. But she'll live."

Ivy was holding the witch's hand, speaking soothing words to her.

"She might need those memories wiped, though," Nerissa added.

"No," said Harker. "I need to know what she knows. I need to know how supernaturals have managed to steal magic that is not their own."

"However it happened, I don't think they can control it," I told him. "Not entirely, at least. It is driving them mad."

"This isn't the first time something like this has happened," he said. "About twenty years ago, the demons gave magic to a group of Earth's supernaturals. They couldn't control it. They went almost primitive, just like you described."

"This isn't demons," I told him.

"How do you know?"

"Ivy didn't find any demon marks on the bodies."

"That just means demons weren't possessing them," he said. "Demons could have still given them magic."

"The source of their magic—the elemental, the vampire, and the werewolf—was light magic, not dark magic."

His eyes hardened. "Is there any point in asking you how you know that?"

"Light magic and dark magic both hurt when they hit

you, but they feel different. They buzz at a different frequency as they tear through your body."

Harker looked at me like he didn't buy it.

But it was true. Light and dark magic did feel different. Plus, I'd seen the difference using dark magic against the vampire and werewolf had made. It had hurt them when my light magic had done nothing.

"Their powers come from light magic. I can feel it." I looked at my team. "Tell him."

"Much as I want to comply, they didn't feel any different to me. Light or dark, I can't tell the difference." Drake shrugged.

"Same," said Alec. "I believe you, Leda, but I didn't feel it. I didn't even know there was a difference."

"There is a difference," Harker said to my surprise. "But only angels can feel it."

Alec leaned back and looked at my back to check for wings. Or maybe he just wanted an excuse to stare at my ass.

"Oh, that's right." I snapped my fingers. "I forgot to tell you all that I became an angel when no one was looking."

"Really?" A spark of hope flashed in Alec's eyes. He was obviously excited by the idea of me as an angel.

I frowned at him. "No. Of course not."

"Let's focus." Harker gave me a chiding look. "You're sure their magic was light magic?"

"Why don't you hunt them down and let them hit you? Then you can see for yourself." I grinned at him.

Harker rubbed his head, his brows drawing together with strained patience. "Not now, Leda. I'm not in the mood for insubordination."

"I'm not insubordinate," I protested. "I'm just wicked."

A smile broke Harker's mouth, despite himself. He covered it up immediately, but I'd already seen it.

"Maybe you should ask the gods where these renegade supernaturals got their powers," I suggested.

Harker frowned. I was pushing him too hard. But it was the truth.

"I know you are not accusing the gods of causing this," he said quietly.

"Do you know of anyone else with the power to give the supernaturals these abilities?"

Harker bit his lip. He knew I had a point. But he stubbornly persisted in his denial. "It makes no sense. The gods are our protectors. They would not do anything to endanger the Earth's citizens."

He was wrong about that. Centuries ago, the gods had turned the Earth into a battleground between them and demons. They'd released monsters onto the Earth. They'd raised an army, the Legion of Angels, giving us powers to counter their enemies. And fight their battles.

I'd stood in the gods' court, played their games, seen them bicker and make rulings based solely on their mood at the time, or based on how most to annoy the gods they were fighting. And I'd watched them discuss humanity with all the indifference of a farmer speaking about the animals he raised for slaughter. They absolutely would do this if the situation suited them.

"Regardless of who is behind this, we need to put a swift end to it," declared Harker. "When the demons struck last time, the Legion killed all the tainted supernaturals infected by their power, but not before the death count was in the thousands. We need to head this off sooner this time."

I remembered what Nero had said, that Harker was under pressure to prove himself, to prove that he could be an effective angel. He couldn't afford a catastrophe in which thousands of people died.

"You are good at tracking people down," Harker said to me in an ode to my days hunting down criminals. "Find the tainted supernaturals."

"It doesn't take a genius to track them down," I told him. "You just follow the trail of blood and destruction. But what are we supposed to do when we find them? They are immune to everything we've got."

"Everyone has a weakness. We just need to find it. And we can start by figuring out how this happened." He looked at Nerissa. "Have you learned anything from the elemental's body?"

"There are no traces of Nectar or Venom in her blood."

Harker gave me a victorious look. Ok, so the gods hadn't done it—this time. But that didn't mean they wouldn't do it. Harker might be blinded by his faith in the gods, but my eyes were wide open. They'd tried to turn my death into a lesson for Nero. Experiences like that tended to give a person a unique perspective into the gods' minds.

"Other than the absence of Nectar and Venom, I don't know anything useful yet," Nerissa continued. "I need to study the body further. It would help if I had more samples. Live samples." She looked at me.

"If you could tell me what hurts them, I might be able to get you one," I told her. "But they seem to become more resilient with every passing moment."

"I'll do my best. At this point, I can't even figure out how this change was possible. I have no idea where they got all this magic. I need time."

"You don't have time," Harker told her.

Nerissa sighed. "Tell me something I don't know."

Leaving the witch in Ivy's care, she turned her attention to Drake. He had a serious bite from the vampire. She swiped the wound and dropped the sample into a vial.

Then she healed Drake's wound with a few drops of potion.

"Go back to your room to rest and recover," she ordered him.

"Hey, I need him. Where am I going to find someone for my team who possesses both muscle and a sense of humor?" I teased.

"I take issue with that," protested Alec. "I possess both muscle and humor in generous quantities."

"I'll be back before you know it," Drake told me, then he left the room.

Nerissa looked at the hole in Alec's shirt.

A smile curled his lips. "Checking me out, Doc?"

"No." She peeled back the torn leather to look at the skin beneath. "There's no wound, but I can tell there used to be," she said, wiping away the blood. "What happened?"

"The vampire pushed a pole through me."

"And your body healed that wound?"

"Leda healed it with some funky powder that made my insides feel like they were imploding."

Nerissa's fingers brushed across a bite wound on his arm. "It looks like a vampire bite. It's not serious."

"Of course not. I knocked the bloodsucker against a building before he could drink from me."

Nerissa poured a potion over the wound.

"What is the matter with you two?!" Alec howled.

"I am simply healing you," Nerissa said serenely.

"It didn't look like it hurt so much when you healed Drake."

"Maybe Drake is just tougher than you are."

Alec scowled at her.

"I need theories. Any theories," Harker said to Nerissa.

He sounded stressed, strained. He knew Nero was evaluating him. And I knew Harker genuinely didn't want anyone to get hurt. He believed the gods were protecting humanity too. I wasn't sure anything could rob him of that delusion.

"The absence of Nectar or Venom doesn't mean the gods or demons aren't interfering," said Nerissa. "Supernaturals don't have Nectar or Venom in them, but they do have magic. It's just there's never been anyone with the powers of multiple supernaturals, not besides a soldier of the Legion or a soldier of hell. We didn't think such a feat was possible without Nectar or Venom."

"It isn't possible for long. They eventually lose their minds." I chewed on that thought. "Maybe the powers aren't the purpose of this. Maybe they are only a side effect. Maybe the insanity and out-of-control supernaturals wreaking havoc is the point."

"You think this is an attack?" Harker asked me.

I shrugged. "It sure as hell isn't a present. An attack is as good a theory as any."

"How was this condition spread?" He looked at Nerissa.

"A poison perhaps. Or a disease."

"So this condition could be contagious?"

Glass shattered. Charlotte the witch had jumped up onto the counter, displacing glass beakers. She launched herself off the table at Alec and slapped him hard across the room. She was strong. Too strong. Elemental magic burst out of her.

Harker and I ducked behind a table.

"It appears the condition is contagious," I said to him.

"And you brought this here, to my office," he hissed at me.

"How was I supposed to know? Honestly, you really can't make up your mind. First, you want us to bring in people for questioning, and then you don't."

"This isn't funny, Pandora."

"I'm not laughing, Harker."

I peeked over the table and shot a bolt of dark lightning at Charlotte. The witch stumbled back, hissing in pain. My second attack, however, didn't push her back as far.

"This is the beginning of the transformation," I commented. "Her power is ramping up. We need to contain her before she grows too powerful."

Lightning shot off of Charlotte in every direction. More beakers shattered as lights exploded overhead. Tables and chairs tumbled over. The witch bolted for the window.

"She's trying to get away!" I shouted.

Ivy jumped up, calling out, "Charlotte!"

The witch hesitated for just a moment. It was enough. Nero rushed into the room, grabbing her by the collar.

"This witch is bizarrely strong," he commented with perfect calmness as she kicked her legs wildly, trying to get free. He pushed the air out of the witch's lungs until she passed out.

Nero turned to Harker. "Is this how you run my office?" he demanded.

Harker didn't dispute that this was his office now. He wiped the blood from his lip. Then he grabbed the sleeping witch and dropped her on Nerissa's desk.

"Here. You have your live sample now," he told her. "Study the change in action. Figure this out."

17

LEADERS OF THE SUPERNATURAL WORLD

*T*he next morning, I woke up early to spend a few hours running on the track. It was good training, but that wasn't the only reason I did it. It also helped me think.

If you have enough energy to think, you aren't pushing your-self hard enough.

That's what Nero would have said if he were here. But he wasn't here. He was probably with Harker, watching how he handled the catastrophe wreaking havoc on the city. There hadn't been any more sightings of crazed supernaturals. Yet.

As I ran, I listened to yesterday's recordings from the Sea King's office and thought about what to do next. Since I'd bugged his office, the Sea King had met with one of his people, but I didn't hear anything useful. The meeting had happened outside of his office.

I finished my last lap, then I headed over to Nerissa's lab. The place was a mess. There were coffee cups piled every-where, most of them half-full. It was as though Nerissa had made coffee to stay awake, then she'd forgotten all about it until she took a sip and realized it was cold. Then she'd made another cup, and the cycle repeated. Over and over again, all night long.

Open folders were scattered everywhere, interspersed with pages of notes and formulas. There were even doodles on some of them. Medical instruments were not put away properly. Nerissa was usually more orderly than this. She was obviously stressed.

I didn't see her in the lab. I did see the witch Charlotte stuck in a cell designed to hold an angel. It was the same sort of Magitech used to power the barriers that kept out the monsters, the ones that separated the civilized lands from the wilds.

Except the Magitech barriers were powered by huge generators. I wondered how big the generators for these prison cells were. They had to be a lot smaller.

The city barriers were like tanks. It took a lot to knock them out. I had only seen one go down once, when Nero and I had sent hundreds of monsters at it. The monsters had died, but the impact had overloaded the barrier. I wondered if these prison cells were equally powerful.

The magic the witch was throwing at it sure was powerful. The barrier didn't seem to notice. I guessed that answered my question.

As I passed by the cell, the witch stopped moving and stared at me. Her eyes were glued to my hair.

"How did you do that?"

I jumped in surprise. I'd been so distracted by the eerie gleam in the witch's eyes that I hadn't noticed Nerissa walk up to me.

She looked…well, terrible. Dark circles hung under her eyes. Her clothes were wrinkled, her hair disheveled, like she'd been running her hands through it constantly all night long.

"How did I do what?" I asked her.

"Get her to stop thrashing and wailing and hitting the barrier with that blasted magic of hers."

"I don't know. She saw my hair and stopped."

Nerissa stared at me. "You have some weird hair, Leda."

"I know." I sighed.

"She's been at it all night, slamming her magic against the barrier nonstop. Driving me so crazy, I could hardly think."

"You've been up all night?"

"Yes."

Maybe that was the real reason she couldn't think. That and her overconsumption of cold coffee.

"Our illustrious new lieutenant colonel wants results," she explained.

"And?"

Nerissa blinked at me. It was a slow blink, like she'd fallen asleep for a second in between.

"Do you have any updates?" I asked her.

"Of course I don't have anything," Nerissa snapped at me. "If I had anything, I would have called you and then treated myself to a nap."

I forgave her because she hadn't slept at all last night. And because she was usually so good-natured.

"You have no ideas?" I asked, surprised. "You always have ideas."

"Is that supposed to be funny?"

"No, it's supposed to be true. You always know everything."

Nerissa scowled at me. "Well, I don't know this. Haven't got a clue. Supernaturals with all the powers of a Legion soldier, but with no sign of Nectar or Venom in their blood. And no sign of demon possession. I've never seen anything like it."

She looked ready to collapse.

"Go to bed," I ordered her.

"Sorry, sweet pea, I already have my orders from an angel. Harker says I need to figure this out now."

"Well, Harker isn't here right now."

I hoped I wasn't jinxing it. This was the perfect time for Harker to stride in and declare that he was, in fact, here. When that didn't happen, I took it as a divine sign for me to continue.

"And if you don't get some rest, you'll never figure out anything," I told her. "There are other scientists. Call Dr. Mackenzie."

"He's in London right now."

"Dr. Martinelli?"

"She's in Chicago."

"Well, there has to be *someone* around. Call them, get some breakfast, and then report your ass to bed."

"Harker will have your head for this," she warned me.

"You let me worry about Harker. You worry about getting some food and rest, so that brilliant intellect of yours can solve this mystery."

"Well, I am brilliant." Nerissa looked somewhat appeased.

I pushed her toward the door. As I left the lab, I pulled out my phone and messaged Ivy.

Nerissa was up all night. I sent her to Demeter. Could you make sure she gets something to eat and then goes to bed?

Ivy responded immediately. *No problem.*

I might as well talk to Harker now. I headed down the hall toward his office, but he found me before I got there.

"Hi," I said with a pleasant smile.

A suspicious crinkle formed between his eyes. "What did you do?"

Busted. I'd just shooed Nerissa out of her lab. He couldn't have found out already.

I smiled wider. "What makes you think I did something?"

He gave me a flat look. "The innocent expression on your face was a dead giveaway."

"That's ridiculous."

"Is it?"

"I was just coming to see you," I told him.

"Well, isn't this fortuitous." His voice had a hard edge to it. In fact, he looked almost as bad as Nerissa. I wondered how much he'd slept last night.

"And?" he demanded. "What do you have for me?"

"Nothing yet."

He frowned. "You were looking for me to say you have nothing."

"Not yet. But I'm going to take the team out again and track down the vampire and werewolf, so they're not on the streets. I just had an idea. I need a portable Magitech generator like the one used in the angel cell holding the witch. I'm going to use it to trap the vampire and the werewolf."

"It's not a bad idea. I'll give one to the team I'm sending after them."

"You're taking me off the mission?"

"I am disappointed in your and Nerissa's lack of progress."

I could tell he was frustrated with this whole thing, especially with how bad it looked to have it happening in his territory during his first week as an angel.

"But this problem is baffling everyone," he continued. "I still think if anyone can solve it, you can." He started walking. "Come with me."

I followed him down the hall. "Where are we going?"

"To the ballroom."

"Because this is the perfect time to dance?"

"No."

He opened the double doors to the ballroom. I'd only ever been in here when it was decorated for a party. Right now, it looked so plain. There were no decorations, music, or party appetizers. Instead, there were only a few boring conference tables—and seated behind them was an unhappy assortment of elementals, witches, vampires, and shifters.

"You already know the Sea King," Harker said. "These are his counterparts, the leaders of the elemental clans: the Fire King, the Sky Queen, and the Earth King. I believe you also know the witch coven leader Constantine Wildman, who is also the head of Zoology at the New York University of Witchcraft. Those are his two aides."

A warm, happy feeling sparked inside of me when I saw that one of the aides was my sister Bella. It had been far too long since we'd hung out. Unfortunately, I feared we wouldn't have much time to chat.

Harker indicated the table where the vampires sat. "These are the leaders of two vampire houses in New York: House Vermillion and House Snowfire."

From the way they were sitting on far ends of the same table, the two vampires didn't get along all that well. Vermillion was the house that was good at reforming rogue vampires. I didn't know much about Snowfire, but the name sounded familiar.

"And the shifters have sent Stash." He looked at Stash sitting alone at the shifter table. "Is that your first or last name?"

"It's my only name."

"These are the leaders of the supernatural groups with members who've been affected by the contagion." Harker looked from me to them. "You are all going to figure this out. Together. Your assets have been frozen until you do."

On that cheerful note, he left the room, closing the door behind him.

None of the supernatural leaders looked happy to be here. I sure wasn't happy about the mess Harker had dumped in my lap either. But maybe some of them knew something that would help us solve this problem. If only I could find a way to make these bickering supernatural leaders work together. They were already arguing. Angry accusations flew across the room.

I sighed and considered the representatives the supernaturals of New York had sent me.

The witches had sent a coven leader, one of the heads of the university. He was a witch of great power, positioned well within the witch community. That told me the witches took this threat very seriously.

Constantine Wildman's aides were dressed in tight corsets and little ballet skirts. They didn't have computers or other gadgets on them. He'd obviously brought them along to serve as human props, to make him look good. Poor Bella. She was too smart to be wasted like this.

The elementals had sent the four elemental leaders. They were arguing amongst themselves; they obviously didn't trust one another. I guessed that was why they'd all come. They wanted to keep an eye on one another.

Stash stood from his seat and walked over to me. He must have noticed how lost I looked.

"Good to see you, Leda. Sorry it had to be under these circumstances," he said.

"What are you doing here?"

"Same as the others. Representing my kind in this collaborative effort."

"I thought you had no connections to the New York City packs."

"I don't, but shifters don't get along well with other packs. The city packs are divided. They couldn't decide on a representative, so they sent me as a neutral party. Ironic, isn't it? They have to count on the person they'd rejected."

"I'm surprised you agreed to come."

He shrugged. "They paid me enough."

My gaze panned across the room of bickering supernaturals. "They couldn't pay me enough to deal with them."

"That's the great thing about being a soldier in the Legion of Angels. You don't get to say no." He patted me on the shoulder, then took his seat again.

I frowned at the leaders of the supernatural world. They were so petty, fighting their own kind, fighting other supernatural kinds. I'd been right the first time. Harker was definitely punishing me.

I put my fingers in my mouth and whistled.

That got their attention. They all stopped and stared at me. The vampires had their hands over their ears. Well, it looked like I'd found a new weapon against them.

"You all know why we are here," I addressed the crowd.

The Snowfire vampire pointed his skinny finger at the Vermillion vampire. "Because one of his vampires killed two Legion soldiers. That's what he gets for taking in stray vampires and not watching them properly."

"We take special care to watch all rogue vampires," the Vermillion vampire replied calmly.

"Then explain last night's massacre."

"That was not a wild vampire."

"So that was one of your regular vampires?" The Snowfire leader clicked his tongue in disapproval.

"We were not the only ones hit by this." The Vermillion

vampire pointed at the elementals. "This infection started with them."

The elementals shouted back. Soon, everyone in the room was shouting.

I clenched my teeth. How was I going to get these bickering supernatural leaders to work together when they couldn't even last five seconds without getting into a fight?

18

WITCHES AND ANGELS

*A*fter spending several hours cooped up with the illustrious leaders of the supernatural world, I dismissed the meeting for lunch. They'd spent the whole morning fighting. I left the room, feeling more exhausted than I did after a day of hard training. Politics were definitely not for me.

Bella and I walked together to the canteen. I had never before looked forward to lunch as much as I did right now. It wasn't about the food. It was about getting away from those bickering, childish supernatural rulers.

Spending a few minutes with my sister was the icing on the cake. She was the only bright spot in this whole mess of a situation.

Demeter was packed. It seemed everyone had gotten hungry at the same time today. Claudia and Basanti were sitting with their initiates, who looked as exhausted as I felt.

"They look so…scared," I commented to Bella. "That was me not so long ago, caught in a fight for my life. A fight I wasn't sure I would win."

"And how does it look from the other side now that you're older and wiser?" she asked me.

"I'm not out of the woods yet. In fact, I feel like I'm going in deeper and deeper."

She looped her arm with mine. "It's always darkest right before dawn."

"See, that's why I love you so much, Bella. You see only the beauty in the world." I glanced at the initiates. "Some things are different from the other side. Nero never sat with us. Harker sometimes did back then. He wouldn't do it now. Angels have to keep their distance, you know. To be unattainable. They are as close as most people get to a god." I looked across the room. Nero sat at the head table next to Harker. "Don't tell Nero I compared him to a god. It's not good for his ego."

"As always, your secrets are safe with me."

Pasta was on the menu today. It smelled great, but when I took a bite, I hardly tasted it. My mind was too distracted.

"What does Constantine Wildman know about this situation?" I asked Bella.

"I don't know. He doesn't share anything with us." She poked at her pasta. "When I was chosen to be one of only two aides on an important assignment, I thought he was choosing the best witches. But I'm starting to think now that he just wanted eye candy."

"Well, you are the prettiest witch I know."

"*Silent* eye candy," she added. "He's encouraged us to smile and never to speak. Or to think too much. He says thinking will only give us wrinkles."

"Well, isn't he a tool."

"If he knows anything about what's going on, he certainly hasn't told us."

"Constantine Wildman is a misogynous pig, but he's a

brilliant witch," Marina Kane said as she joined us at our table.

Bella gave her friend's hand a squeeze. "How are you holding up here?"

Just a short while ago, Marina had attended the New York University of Witchcraft with Bella. But the Legion's Interrogators had manipulated her into joining our ranks. It was either that or her coven and everyone in it would be disgraced. She'd sacrificed her future for theirs.

"No one ever said joining the Legion of Angels was easy," Marina said. "Well, joining is easy. It's surviving that's hard."

"I can't believe they coerced you into enlisting."

"Come on, Bella," I said. "You're smart. You know the Legion."

My sister sighed. "You're right. I can believe it."

"I'll be fine." Marina leaned in, dipping her voice to a soft whisper. "I've heard about your problem."

"As always, news travels fast at the Legion."

"All of New York's supernaturals are talking about it. They're calling it Angel Fever," she told me. "Because the affected supernaturals are gaining the abilities of angels."

"They're also gaining insanity," I pointed out.

"Some people say it's worth the price. And some think they could control it if they were infected."

"They couldn't," I told her.

"You're probably right," agreed Marina. "There's no hope of controlling this. But there are a lot of arrogant supernaturals. Word's gotten out that the condition is contagious. Some people have begun to seek out the infected, trying to catch whatever it is they have."

Harker would have *loved* that. How the hell did anyone find out so much about this disease? If that was even what it was.

"I wouldn't be surprised if some of the leaders who've come here know something about it," Marina said. "Maybe one of them was responsible."

None of the supernatural leaders had that kind of power. In fact, no one short of a deity had that kind of power. But then again, no one really understood everything about magic. So never say never. Centuries ago, no one thought monsters would overrun the lands as a war played out on Earth between gods and demons. Hell, people hadn't even known magic existed back then.

"How do you know all of this?" I asked her.

"I might not be a witch anymore, but I still have connections. I hear things."

She froze when she saw Harker walking toward us. Her heart might have even stopped when he sat down beside me. She must have never been this close to an angel before.

"If you're interested, there's a trick for getting an angel's wings to come out," I told her. "You touch them just between the shoulder blades and then…"

"Careful, Pandora," Harker warned me. "Nero is watching. And if you flirt with me, he'll tear my arm out of my socket."

"I am not flirting with you. I'm merely sharing my expertise on angels with my friends."

Harker looked amused. "Expertise?"

"Yes, expertise," I repeated. "And don't get your wings in a twist. Nero knows I love only him." I looked across the room and winked at my angel.

Nero's lips turned up, ever so slightly.

Marina didn't meet Harker's eyes. She looked down at her hands. So the confident witch was shy around angels.

I looked at Harker. "Now see what you've done. You've scared her."

"Believe it or not, Leda, I scare off a lot of women nowadays. Apparently, angels are intimidating."

I snorted. "No kidding. Having regrets that you became an angel, are you?"

"No. The benefits outweigh the costs."

"It sure would be useful to be able to fly." If I were an angel, I could have flown away instead of going back to that meeting chamber.

"I can take you flying sometime if you want," Harker offered.

"Na, you'd probably drop me."

Harker looked offended. "I would never do such a thing."

"So, did you come over here for smalltalk, or do you have another reason for gracing us with your angelic presence?" I asked him.

"You know why I'm here, Leda."

"You want an update on the Council of Unfortunate Supernaturals."

"Yes."

"Well, I got them to stop fighting. And then it was lunch time." I patted him on the shoulder. "Consider yourself updated."

Harker frowned. "I asked about your progress. Are you telling me you got absolutely nothing accomplished?"

"The supernatural leaders don't get along."

"They don't have to get along. It's your job to make them obedient. And to see if any of them know anything. I expect a report by the end of the day."

He rose, then his gaze shifted to Bella. "You are Leda's sister."

"I am," she said coolly.

"Has she always been so frustrating?"

"It depends on who you ask," Bella replied.

Harker laughed. "I'm asking you."

"Then you're out of luck. I don't tattle on my sister." She frowned at him. "Not even to angels."

I'd never seen her so cold with anyone. She was usually so friendly.

"I see." Harker looked at me. "The report is due at midnight, Pandora. And you'd better have something illuminating to put in it."

I watched him leave, frustrated.

"He is so hot," Marina muttered when Harker was sitting back at the head table.

"It doesn't matter how hot he is. No one treats my sister like that," Bella said, steel in her voice.

So that was why she'd been so cold to him.

Marina didn't seem to hear Bella. She was too busy staring at Harker.

The bell chimed, and I stood. "Time to return to the battlefield."

"You mean the ballroom," Bella corrected me.

I shook my head. "No. I really mean the battlefield."

***

THE AFTERNOON SESSION OF THE COUNCIL OF Unfortunate Supernaturals didn't prove any more fruitful than the morning session had. I left the ballroom at the end of the day, my ears still ringing from the hours of insults the supernatural leaders had hurled at each other like children throwing food in a high school cafeteria.

Ivy and Drake were sitting on the sofa in our living room, getting ready to start a movie.

"Leda, you're just in time," Ivy said. "You can help us

pick the movie. Which should it be: *The Witch Covens of Sleepy Hollow*, or *Vampires vs. Werewolves*?"

"I had quite enough of Vampires vs. Werewolves last night."

Drake looked at Ivy. "I agree."

"*The Witch Covens of Sleepy Hollow*, it is." Ivy turned the disc over in her hand. "I'm not sure if this film is a love story or a horror movie."

"I think it's both," Drake told her.

Ivy grinned at him. "That's the best kind. Remember back in eighth grade when our parents went out of town and we watched *The Vampire Hunter* trilogy?"

"Sure I do, but I'm surprised you remember." Mischief sparked in his eyes. "You spent most of the trilogy hiding your head under the blanket in terror."

"That was you, genius."

"No, I distinctly remember it was a girl with red pigtails."

She tossed a few pieces of popcorn at him. He caught them all in his mouth, one after the other. But he swallowed too fast and choked on a kernel.

Ivy snorted, thumping him on the back. She looked at me. "Come on, join us, Leda. We have popcorn."

She and Drake were sure sitting close. And the way they were looking at each other made me realize I needed to be somewhere else—*anywhere* else. Maybe I'd pay Nerissa a visit.

"How is Nerissa doing?" I asked Ivy.

"She got some sleep this morning and now she's back at work," Ivy told me. "She looks worlds better. But she kicked me out of her lab so she could concentrate. She kicked out everyone else too. We're all banned. She promised to give us Dragon Pox if we returned before morning."

Ok, maybe I wouldn't pay Nerissa a visit after all. She

obviously wasn't in a talking mood. Dragon Pox weren't deadly, but they were really itchy.

"I'm going to head to the library," I decided. "I need a quiet space to write my report for Harker."

"What you need is your own office."

"I certainly do."

They turned on the movie as I walked out. Ivy and Drake seemed to be slowly realizing how they feel about each other. They just needed some time alone so they could take the plunge.

And I needed to find a way to fill several pages with text. I didn't have anything to tell Harker. I had no clue what Angel Fever was, no clue how it had started, and no clue how it was spreading. On top of all that, I also had no clue how to stop it. How the hell was I going to expand that to five pages? I was definitely going to need a really big font.

One thing I did know was the infection was spreading. And if supernaturals were purposely putting themselves in its path, soon Angel Fever was going to get out of control. If we didn't have a cure before then, more people were going to die.

19

ANGEL FEVER

I woke up early to run the next morning. Two hours later, I still didn't have any new ideas. My bug in the Sea King's office hadn't yielded anything more interesting than a planning session he'd held late last night to organize New York City's annual Water and Ice Ball. The meeting had included a whole lot of tabletop decorations and menu options—but no deep, dark secrets. I was this close to bugging the office of every supernatural leader in the city.

I poked my scrambled eggs in frustration. I was eating breakfast alone this morning. The breakfast rush hadn't yet started.

"Leda." Harker sat down opposite me.

"Good morning," I said brightly. My foster mother Calli had always told me to start off each morning with a smile.

Harker wasn't smiling.

"Well, don't you look cheerful this morning?" I commented. "What's wrong? Didn't you get enough sleep?"

"I read your report before bed."

"That explains it," I said seriously. "Did my vivid descriptions of the battles give you nightmares?"

"Your report was colorful."

"I aim to please."

"Colorful but without substance," he continued. "It read like a teenage soap opera."

"That's what it was in that meeting hall with those supernatural leaders. It's like high school. No, that's too mature for them. It's like a freaking kindergarten."

"Fix this," Harker told me. "Use that creative, out-of-the-box thinking you're famous for."

More like infamous. The Legion was very much in the box—in *their* box.

Harker stood, repeating, "Fix this."

As he walked away, Ivy and Drake sat down beside me. They weren't holding hands or kissing. They were acting like they were still in denial—in other words, the new status quo for them. It seemed nothing had happened after I'd left them last night. I was going to have to resort to extreme measures.

Except I didn't have room in my brain right now for romantic schemes. It was already overloaded trying to figure out Angel Fever. Yep, Marina had been right. The name was spreading fast. And I'd been right too. The angels didn't approve of the term. They didn't appreciate being compared to wild, out-of-control supernaturals.

"How is Charlotte?" I asked Ivy.

"Our witchy guest eventually fell asleep this morning. We gave her a strong sedative to keep her that way. It's worked so far."

"Nerissa must be happy. She said the witch's banging against the barrier was driving her crazy."

"It was driving us all crazy," said Ivy. "You could hear it across the whole floor."

"We could even hear it in the gym last night for target

practice with Alec," Drake added. "It's louder than gunfire. That's just not natural."

"Where is Nerissa now?" I asked.

"In her lab. She kicked me out again. Said I was distracting her by breathing or something. But she's still testing Charlotte's blood. She's determined to find something."

I grabbed Ivy's arm and looked it up and down. "At least she didn't give you Dragon Pox."

"She still might."

Drake rose from his seat. "See you later, ladies. I have to go change for a mission."

"You already have a mission: working for me," I told him.

"Sorry, Leda. Harker's orders. He says it's your job to grill the city's supernatural leaders. He's sending a bunch of us in teams of two to scour the city, looking for wild supernaturals. We're bringing along Magitech traps."

I poked my eggs again. "Well, at least he listened to my idea."

"I figured it was your idea. Those generators aren't exactly portable. I guess that's why no one else thought of using them as traps. But we managed to make them portable. Somewhat."

"Ah, you're carrying them. You're the muscle," I realized.

"You know I am," he replied, grinning. "But those generators are so heavy it takes two of us to carry one. Alec and I are one of the teams."

"Have fun."

"You know I will."

Ivy caught his hand as he stepped back. She met his eyes. "Be careful." When she realized she was holding his hand, she hastily dropped it.

Drake gave her a smile and left.

I smirked at Ivy.

"What?" she asked me.

"You two sure are acting strange this morning," I told her.

"No, we're not." Her voice broke. "Not at all."

"Ok." I went back to eating my eggs.

"There's nothing strange going on," she insisted.

"I said ok."

"Your lips say ok, but your eyes say something else."

I shrugged. "What can I say? I'm a complicated person."

"I'm not going to argue with that. And speaking of complicated, your angel is coming this way."

I turned in my seat. Sure enough, Nero was heading straight for me.

"Hello, stranger," I greeted him as he stopped beside our table.

"I need to speak to you."

"Ok. Sure."

"Come with me."

I stood up, dropping off my tray on the way out of the canteen. We walked the halls in silence.

"I know you're feeling lost, not being familiar with the players in the supernatural community," he finally said.

"They're certainly a lot to take."

"I did this for years. Getting them to behave is a challenge. How are they acting?"

"Petty," I replied.

"They are always petty. What else? Are they scared? Excited?"

"The Sea King is definitely worried about something. Something he doesn't want the other elemental clans to find out about."

"How do you know?" he asked.

I folded my arms across my chest and smiled. "A magician never reveals her secrets."

He stared at me for a moment, then declared, "You bugged his office, didn't you?"

My smile turned upside down. "How did you know?"

"I know you better than you think."

Magic swept across my body, tingling my senses. I couldn't tell if it was his magic or mine.

"What else?" Nero asked me.

"The vampires have been trading insults with the witches. The elementals have been trading insults with one another. And Stash doesn't seem to know anything. The shifters obviously just sent him because they had to send someone. He tries to make the others get along, but there's no hope of that." I paused. "And I hear news has gotten out to the general public about Angel Fever."

"You shouldn't use that name," he said sternly.

"I actually kind of like it. Angel Fever." I let the words roll off my tongue. "I was wondering if I could catch it."

He stopped walking. "Pandora, you already have."

I felt something strange, a hot breath whispering his words across my skin. I realized it was him. His magic. And he wasn't referring to the contagion. He was talking about a different kind of Angel Fever.

I leaned in to him, speaking against his lips, "You know, I think you're right." I looped my arms over his shoulders. My fingers stroked through his hair, hair almost as soft as his feathers.

He captured my hands in his and gave me a hard look. "What do you want?"

"What do you mean?" I put on an innocent face.

"You're not fooling anyone, Pandora."

"What? I can't want to snuggle up to my man?"

"You usually put up more of a fight. You enjoy this game."

My mouth brushed his neck. "So do you."

"Yes." His green eyes swirled with gold and silver magic.

I gave his lip a final nip, then lowered down from my tiptoes. "Fine. I do need your help. I want you to step into that conference room, with your big, badass magic and big, badass body. And I want you to make those supernatural leaders behave themselves."

"That's your assignment," he told me.

"I'm not a diplomat. And they are driving me mad."

"You need to find a way to get through to them, to make cool heads prevail."

"Do you know me at all? *I* don't even have a cool head," I shot back. "And after a day cooped up with them in that room, I'm ready to murder the whole bickering lot of them."

He chuckled. "I'm sure you'll figure it out. Being an angel isn't just about setting your sword on fire and bashing heads. You need to be able to command. You have powerful siren magic. And I've found you can be very convincing."

"If I were so convincing, you would have agreed to help me," I pouted.

"See this as preparation for the next level, as a way to grow your mental magic. Telekinesis is a mental magic skill. You will need a lot of mental control to level up your magic."

"Every challenge in life is an opportunity for more training?"

"Yes."

"See, I have a better idea. An opportunity for you, if you will." I traced my fingertips across the collar of his leather jacket. "You help me, and I'll buy that lacy two-piece you want me to wear."

"You misunderstand, Pandora."

I planted my hands on my hips and smirked at him. "Oh, is that so?"

"Yes. If I wanted you to wear that lingerie, I'd buy it for you, and you'd wear it."

I laughed.

But he wasn't laughing. His mouth was hard, unforgiving. And his eyes burned with cold fire. My laugh caught in my throat, the smile dying on my lips. It was then that I realized he was right. If he told me to wear it, I would.

A feverish heat flushed my skin. Just thinking about it made me want to put it on now. I saw myself in front of him. Nero slipping his hand under the lace, sliding the strap off my shoulder. His mouth dipping to my neck, biting into my soft flesh. A surge of heat cascaded in me, drawing me under.

"Stop," I choked out.

"Stop what?"

"Stop putting those images in my head."

"Could you describe these images?" His voice hummed with a dark and ruthless sensuality. "What am I doing in them?"

I could feel him drinking from me, my pulse synching to his. I arched my back, pressing myself against him. Yearning for his touch.

Hot, heavy breaths puffed out of me. "You are a wicked man...Nero Windstriker."

"And don't you forget it," he whispered into my ear.

The image in my head popped, but the feeling of intense longing lingered on. I was standing there, in the hallway where anyone could see us, my leg wrapped around Nero, my nails drilling into his back. I cleared my throat and stepped away from him.

Nero leaned down and kissed me softly on the lips. "I have work to do. See you later."

Then he turned and walked back down the hall, leaving me in that raw, senseless state of arousal. He loved playing games all right.

"I'm going to get you for this," I called out to him. Then I took a deep breath and entered Nerissa's lab.

She sat behind her desk, bent over her computer. She was so absorbed in her work that I had to call out her name a few times before she looked up. On the bright side, at least that meant she hadn't seen or heard me and Nero making out outside her office.

"How's it coming?" I asked, trying to clear my head of Nero. Except thoughts of my revenge. I was going to get him good.

"These samples from the infected supernaturals are baffling," Nerissa said. "I've never seen anything like Angel Fever."

She'd been stuck in this lab for days, and she *still* knew the name? Well, she wasn't known as the Legion's queen of gossip for nothing.

"The cocktail of supernatural powers in Serenity was positively baffling," Nerissa continued. "That is, until I had a good look at Charlotte. The witch's body is changing. The magic in her blood is changing."

"Evolving?"

"Yes, just like you said. Your instincts were dead on." She rolled her chair to the other end of the desk. A collection of labeled vials were stacked there. "I have been tracking her. She is slowly getting new powers. One-by-one, they are changing her. Sound familiar?"

"Like a Legion soldier gains powers, one by one."

"Yes."

"You're saying that some infection is changing supernaturals' magic like Nectar or Venom does to us?"

"Like I said before, it's not Nectar or Venom. There isn't any of either in their blood. And no natural infection works like this. This is engineered. It is a spell designed to rewrite their magic, very similar to Nectar or Venom."

"But who is behind it?" I asked.

"I don't know."

"How can anyone have this kind of power? And what are they trying to do?"

"I don't know."

My hoped deflated. "Well, let me know if you find out anything else."

I left Nerissa's office, my mind swimming with possibilities. I sure had a lot to mull over. When I entered the ballroom, the supernatural leaders were already trading insults. Or still trading them. I didn't know. Nor did I care. I slammed the door shut behind me.

That got their attention. They stopped bickering and turned to stare at me.

I debated how much I should share with them. The Legion wasn't big into sharing because that tended to tip off the bad guys. But sometimes you had to go against the grain.

"Charlotte, the witch we're holding, has been going through some changes," I announced. "She is gaining powers one-by-one, going madder with each new boost in magic. This isn't a natural occurrence. Someone has engineered it." My eyes panned across my captive audience. "I invite the culprit to step forward and confess. You know the Legion will find out eventually."

Shockingly, no one spoke up. I considered following Nero's suggestion and using my siren magic to compel them. No one was wearing an anti-compulsion amulet today.

The doors to the ballroom burst open and Toren, a guy who'd been in my initiate group, rushed inside. "Angel Fever has spread to the Legion," he told me. "Alec Morrows is infected."

I just stared at him in shock. How could that be? The Nectar in our blood was the poison of all poisons. It should have made us immune to Angel Fever.

"How is Alec handling it?" I asked Toren.

"The angels have him contained. He's obviously trying to fight it, but he's losing the battle."

"Do they know how the spell spreads?"

"They believe it might be spread through blood."

The wild vampire had bitten Alec. Oh, shit. He'd bitten Drake too. I had to check on him. I rushed past Toren, sprinting down the hall and up the staircase. Drake had to be in our apartment. He was going there to change before his mission.

I kept running. Almost there. I zigzagged down the hall-way, cutting around everyone I passed. I reached for the knob.

My apartment door exploded in my face.

20

JUST ANOTHER DAY

I rushed through the missing door into my apartment. Debris littered the floor. The sofa was in pieces. Ivy's lovely moon charm decorations that had amused Nero lay burning on the floor. I stomped out the flames and made my way further inside.

My bedroom door was hanging off its hinges. Pretty much everything inside my room had been destroyed. Pillow feathers floated in the air. Torn shreds of clothing decorated the carpet like confetti. Some of my leather uniforms appeared to be intact. So they didn't just look badass; Legion uniforms could also survive an explosion.

I worked my way through the apartment, looking for Drake. And for Ivy. She always changed out of her sports clothes before going to work. She had to be here somewhere. I had to help her before Drake hurt her.

My eyes felt like there was glass in them. Feathers and dust filled the air like a thick fog, mixing with the wild magic. I choked on the stench.

I followed the sounds of a fight spilling out of Drake's

room. Ivy's voice was strained. She was in pain. I closed in carefully, my sword drawn.

But when I passed into Drake's room, I realized it wasn't Drake who'd been infected. It was Ivy. She was hurling elemental spells she shouldn't possess at him, one after the other. Crazed, tormented by the monsters inside of her mind, she didn't stop.

Drake tried to tackle her to the ground, but he was not aiming to kill. Ivy was. She shot a stream of fire at him, and he ducked behind what remained of his overturned dresser.

I crouched next to him. "How's it going?"

"Oh, you know. My best friend is infected with a contagion that's made her gain scary new magical powers and lose her mind. Just another day at the Legion." He was trying to sound casual, but I could hear the worry in his voice. And the fear.

"We have to knock her out. Then we're going to save her. I promise."

"How do you intend to stop her?" he asked me.

"Do you happen to have that Magitech trap lying around?"

"No. It's in the garage."

"I need you to go get it," I told him.

"It's too heavy for me to move alone. I'll need to find Alec first."

"Alec is infected too. Find someone else to help you carry it."

Drake's expression hardened with determination. "I'll figure out something."

"Go. And hurry. I'll cover your retreat."

As Drake ran away, I leapt over the toppled dresser and shot a swirling ball of dark fire at Ivy. She cringed and jumped back, cradling her burned arm, snarling like a savage wounded animal. If there was something of my friend in there, I didn't see it. I just hoped Nerissa found a cure, so I could get her back.

I hit Ivy with magic again, and I didn't hold back. I knew she could take it. All of the infected supernaturals had resilience to spare. That was the problem.

Ivy hissed at me, patting out the flames in her hair.

"Stings, doesn't it?" I said.

She rushed forward, tackling me. I projected my shifting magic, animating the furniture to look like me. Since the chairs and tables weren't alive, I had to infuse a lot of magic into the spell.

Together with my army of lookalikes, I closed in on Ivy. The shifted furniture couldn't do much besides circle around her, but they were a decent distraction. Ivy froze, perplexed, not sure which of my lookalikes to go after. So she attacked everything that moved. She punched through one of my lookalikes. Shards of wood splintered off of her arm.

A shock ripped through my body when my other self fell. I severed our link, and she turned back into a chair. Ivy was already tearing through another lookalike. This battle was going on too long. I was starting to have trouble maintaining the spell. Nero had told me that shifting people outside your-self was harder than shifting yourself. And shifting non-living beings was harder yet.

Drake ran into the room, carrying the mini-generator on his shoulders.

"You carried it all the way here? Alone?" I said in shock.

"I couldn't wait. Ivy is in danger."

Wow. He really loved her. Who said romance was dead? Too bad Ivy was too out of her mind right now to compre-hend what he'd done for her.

"We need to get the generator closer to her," I told him.

"Do you see how she's not moving out of that spot. It's like she knows this thing will trap her."

Which was weird because the infected people didn't seem to think all that much.

I grabbed one end of the generator. "Gods, Drake. This is even heavier than it looks."

"And you're stronger than you look, Leda."

We ran at Ivy, throwing the generator. She dodged, but the generator was close enough. A golden barrier slid around her like a veil, enclosing her.

Harker and Nero came running into the apartment with a group of soldiers.

"You're late, boys," I told them, dusting off my hands.

The two angels looked at Ivy, who was pounding against the barrier with magic fireworks. The barrier buzzed but held.

"My idea worked," I said to Harker.

"I can see that," he replied. "But unfortunately we don't have an unlimited supply of Magitech generators. How did you trap her?"

"We threw the generator at her and activated it."

"You *threw* the generator at her?" He wasn't able to keep the surprise out of his voice.

I looked at Drake. "Well, Drake helped a little."

"A *little*? Thanks, Leda."

"I trust there's no point in lecturing you about the Legion's policy on throwing expensive machinery?" Harker said.

"Why on Earth would the Legion need a policy on that?"

"Nero implemented one shortly after you joined the Legion."

I looked at Nero.

He shrugged. "You do like to throw things," he pointed out.

"Yeah, water bottles and rocks. Not Magitech generators."

"A preemptive move," Nero said. "I figured it was only a matter of time before you grew strong enough to expand into heavier objects."

I almost laughed. Harker's expression checked that urge.

"So am I getting punished?" I asked.

Nero looked at Harker. Right, it was his call. Nero was just observing. And taking notes for his report. He wouldn't interfere with Harker's decisions, no matter how much he wanted to protect me. Maybe he'd even applaud a little discipline. Nero valued things like order and dignity. He was an angel after all.

"Pick up the generator, Pandora," Harker told me.

I stepped toward it. Drake moved to help me, but Harker cut him off. "Stop. She'll do it alone."

I tried to lift the generator off the ground. It stubbornly refused to cooperate.

I tried again. This time, I succeeded, powered by stubborn will. Ok, so I also drew a little on my bond with Nero for extra strength. I knew he felt it, but he didn't say a thing. That was the great thing about Nero. He let me handle things that I could do alone and helped me without question when I really needed his help. Now was one of those times.

"Bring it to Dr. Harding's lab," Harker said.

"You want me to carry it all the way there?"

Ivy was thrashing above me, adding to the weight I was carrying. It was a good thing the Legion of Angels had buildings with high ceilings or Ivy would have taken out the ceiling. Unfortunately, high ceilings also meant lots of stairs.

"Yes," Harker said as I gaped at the stairwell looming before me. "Down the stairs. It is a good reminder of the consequences of throwing things."

As I walked, that weight pressing down on me, sweat drenching my skin, I muttered, "You won't be so smug when I throw *you*."

"I heard that," Harker told me.

"You were meant to, genius." I resettled the generator's weight when we reached the bottom of the stairs. "I can't believe you carried this thing all the way from the garage," I said to Drake.

"Maybe you need to increase your weight training." He grinned. "Practice with me."

"No thanks. I see the weights you lift. No way." I stumbled, but caught myself before I fell.

"Perhaps instead of smarting off, you should concentrate on the task at hand," Harker said.

"Na, smarting off takes no energy. It's just like breathing."

Harker looked at Nero. "I think I understand why you were complaining about her when she joined the Legion. Her mouth is considerably less charming when I'm in charge."

"Perhaps instead of considering the qualities of her mouth, you should concentrate on the matter at hand," Nero replied coolly.

I smirked at Harker. Haha.

"I'm letting you off easy," he told me.

"You carry this generator, and then you can call it easy."

"I could have punished you more severely. I will overlook your transgression this time because you contained the threat."

"That *threat* is my friend."

"And if we put an end to this plague, she might get to be your friend again."

We entered the lab. Nerissa froze when she saw the enormous generator I was carrying.

"So a city-wide disaster is what it takes for me to finally get the new equipment I've asked for," she commented.

I set down the generator at her feet. "You have a new patient, Doctor."

Nerissa frowned. "And just when I'd finally put the last one to sleep." She watched as Ivy smashed spells against the barrier, doing her best to blast it—and all of us—to smithereens. "So Angel Fever has spread to the Legion."

"*How* is it spreading?" Harker demanded.

"Oh, I've got that figured out." She pulled a handful of syringes out of her cabinet. "It spreads by sound. Every time an infected person uses their magic, the song of that spell spreads."

Sound, huh? Now, that was a new one.

"Song? As in Siren's Song?" I asked. "Could sirens be behind this?"

"Perhaps. The infected people are showing signs of being compelled. But I've never heard of sirens who could bestow people with new abilities," Nerissa told me.

"Are you familiar with the drug the Legion sometimes gives its soldiers before they face hell's army?" Nero asked.

"Yes, it's an anti-compulsion drug." She nodded. "Good idea. I'll try to cook up something." She held up the first syringe. "But first I need to test each of you. I've found the identifying magic in all the infected people, a magic mark in their blood."

She drew blood from Drake first. "Sorry," she said after looking at it under her microscope. "You're infected."

He glanced at Ivy. "How long until it takes me over?"

"I'm not sure. We'd best lock you up just in case."

She tested Nero and Harker next. Both were clear.

"I think angels are unlikely to become infected due to the high amount of Nectar in their blood." She looked up from her microscope and gave me a strange look.

"What?" I asked. It was my blood she was looking at now. "Do I have cooties?"

"You're clear. But you have an unusually high Nectar count in your blood. And it's coupled with... *Venom.*"

"Oh." I tried to make my response as noncommittal as possible.

"Nectar and Venom, intertwined. I've never seen anything like it before." She chewed on her lower lip. "It could be the infection in a mutated form."

"No, she's clear," Nero told her.

"How do you know?"

"Because we're linked, so I would know if her magic were infected."

"So you're saying she's...always been like this?" Nerissa began mixing potion ingredients over a small cauldron.

Harker was watching us all very closely.

"You witnessed what she did at Storm Castle, draining the Venom from Basanti. Surviving it. You must have already realized what it meant," Nero said.

"Yes." Harker looked at me. "You can wield both light and dark magic."

Some considered that a magical impossibility. The gods would call it blasphemy.

"What are you going to do about it?" I asked him. "Wait, no. Don't answer that. I'm not sure I can believe the answer."

"I never meant to hurt you, Leda. I would never do that."

His eyes darted to Nero. "Are you going to put that in your report?"

"No."

"This is remarkable." Nerissa held up a vial of sparkling liquid. It looked like carbonated water. "I've used Leda's magic to create something that will hold off the effects of the contagion, at least until her magic breaks down inside the potion. The dark and light mix does a marvelous job of confusing Angel Fever, making it unable to connect."

"So I'm immune?" I asked her.

"Yes. If only my potion made other people immune too. It's not a cure, but it is a temporary fix. The true cure to the condition is Nectar, but that cure would kill the infected person." She injected a dose of the potion into her own arm. "But my potion will buy us time to find a true cure."

"How long?" Harker asked.

"A few hours at most."

Which meant we had very little time.

Bella ran into the lab. "Leda," she said, breathless.

"Bella, great timing," I replied. "We have something that might hold off the Angel Fever. At least for a little while. Bring the supernatural leaders here so we can inoculate them."

"Stash, half the elementals, and Heather, Constantine Wildman's other aide, just jumped through the ballroom's windows," she said.

"They're infected?"

She nodded.

"We have to get them back before they spread the infection," I told everyone.

"It's too late for that, Leda."

"What do you mean?" I asked her.

"Come with me and see for yourselves."

We followed her upstairs, onto the big tiled terrace on the roof. From here, we had a pretty good view of the city. Supernaturals had flooded the streets, running faster than a train, streaming like a river out of the city. And they were all heading toward the Black Plains.

21

THE SUPERNATURAL ARMY

I watched the infected supernaturals leave the city, running fast toward the Black Plains like a river of lost souls. I wasn't sure if their departure was good or bad. At least it meant Angel Fever wouldn't continue to spread inside the city. But why were they leaving? Whoever was controlling them must have had a reason to engineer this magical infection—a reason beyond mere mass hysteria. Was summoning them onto the Black Plains just the next stage in this master plan? Was it an omen of a great war to come?

Harker had ordered our building to be locked down. Now that Angel Fever had spread to the Legion, we didn't want to add our numbers to the collective might of the swelling army outside.

"It's taking longer for the magic contagion to infect our soldiers than it did to infect other supernaturals, thanks to the amount of Nectar in our blood. And our willpower," Nerissa said when we returned to her lab. "The higher a soldier's rank, the longer it takes for Angel Fever to set in."

Harker frowned at her. "We agreed we weren't using that name."

"*You* agreed that Harker," Basanti said as she entered the room.

"I'm in charge."

"I don't think anyone is in charge of this situation." Basanti looked at Nero. "The building is fully locked down."

"Good," he replied. "You, Leda, Harker, and I will follow the army to the Black Plains to assess the threat."

Bella walked into the lab with the two vampires, Constantine Wildman, the Sea King, and the Fire King.

Harker shot them a look loaded with nightmare promises. "If any of you know what's going on, speak now."

The supernatural leaders remained stubbornly silent.

"He knows something." I looked at the Sea King.

The leader of the city's water and ice elementals lifted his hands in feigned innocence. "I know nothing."

I pulled out my phone.

"We have a problem," the Sea King's voice spoke out of the speakers. "We need to deal with it before the other elementals find out—or worse yet, the Legion. Tell Holden to come to me."

I paused the recording, smiling at him.

"I…"

"Before the other elementals find out?" the Fire King repeated, his jaw clenched. "Now look what your secrets have cost us."

Harker's hard gaze fell on me. "You bugged his office without asking for my approval."

"We're beyond that now, don't you think? This problem has escalated too far," I pointed out. "A magical contagion has infected hundreds of supernaturals, including the Legion's own soldiers, and you're worried about procedure?"

Harker just shook his head slowly. He looked at the Sea King and said, "What do you know?"

"We'd noticed some changes in Serenity and in some other elementals before the Tsunami Incident," the Sea King admitted.

The Tsunami Incident. That was what it was being called now.

"We locked away the others, but we didn't get to her fast enough." His gaze darted nervously between Harker and Nero. "I swear I don't know anything else."

"There's no time for a thorough interrogation to see if he's lying," said Nero.

"My gut tells me he's telling the truth," I said.

"As does mine," Nero agreed.

Harker turned to the other supernatural leaders. "What about the rest of you? Now is the time to come forward and confess your sins."

"This is not our work," the Vermillion vampire insisted. "We don't wave our hands around and conjure spells." He looked pointedly at the two elementals.

Fire erupted on the Fire King's hands.

"Put out that fire," Harker told him.

The Fire King continued to glare at the vampire through his orange flames.

Harker repeated his order.

"See what I've had to deal with?" I told him.

Harker ignored me. His hard eyes drew together, burning with wrath. "Put it out."

I could see his siren's magic working on the Fire King. The flames on the elemental's hands went out.

"Now, sit down," Harker told him.

The Fire King sat in one of Nerissa's chairs. The other leaders followed suit, before Harker could turn his fury on them.

"Some of you have withheld information," he said.

The vampire tried to speak, but Harker silenced him.

"Withholding that information from the Legion is what allowed this situation to blow up. The Legion's Interrogators will sort it out later, after we've cleaned up this mess. We're heading for the Black Plains now. We're going to follow that army to its source. And you are all coming with us."

"The Black Plains are no place for civilized people," the Snowfire vampire protested.

"Coward," Constantine Wildman chided him.

The vampire bared his fangs at the witch. "This is suicide. What is to stop the infection from getting us too? Then this will all be for nothing."

"I have a potion to protect you against the effects of Angel Fever," Nerissa said. "At least for a while."

She didn't tell them that the potion was made from my blood. I didn't know if that would excite or repulse them, but I was glad she was keeping it a secret.

"The stronger your will, the longer this potion will help you resist the effects of Angel Fever," she told them.

"That means the vampires won't last long. They are such physical, savage creatures." Constantine Wildman turned up his nose at them.

The Snowfire vampire launched himself at the witch. Harker froze him midair with a telekinetic wave.

The Fire King chose that fine moment to lose his mind. Fire flamed up on his hands. He swung his fiery fists, hitting the Snowfire vampire hard. Too hard for an elemental. Here we went again.

I looked at Nero, who nodded at me. I ran over to the cell holding Charlotte. Nero blasted the Fire King with a psychic burst. I slammed my hand against the controls, lowering the barrier just long enough for Nero's magic to knock him into the cell. Then I pounded the button again, and the gold barrier zipped back up over the cell.

The Fire King jumped to his feet. He blasted the barrier with magic once, then he fell unconscious to the floor. I'd shot him with one of Nerissa's magic tranquilizers on his way into the cell.

"You four *will* join us in our mission on the Black Plains," Nero told the four remaining supernatural leaders.

Harker looked at Nerissa, Bella, and Marina. "You three stay here to work on a cure."

"There's no guarantee we will find one," Nerissa told him.

"Just try your best," Nero said. "Slow the spread as much as you can with your potions." He looked at the rest of us. "Now let's go hunt down whoever is controlling the swarm."

I STOOD ON THE AIRSHIP'S UPPER DECK, LOOKING DOWN on the Black Plains. As the name suggested, the lands were black, scorched as though hellfire had rolled across them, burning everything in its path. Even centuries later, there was nothing left. Nothing but the twisted plants and savage beasts that now reigned supreme in these wild lands.

Even the air smelled like ash. I coughed. No matter how many times I visited this place, it just didn't grow on me.

"You have lovely hair," the Snowfire vampire commented, watching as the wind blew my hair across my face. He reached for it.

I blocked his hand. "You touch my hair, and I'll cut off your hand."

"You don't have it in you, a sweet thing like you."

I drew my sword and launched myself off the floor, slashing out with my blade. A small flying monster, about the

193

size of a turkey, dropped dead to the deck. I plucked it off the wood planks and tossed it at the Snowfire vampire with a smirk. He caught the dead bird, speechless.

I leaned over to wipe the blood off his cheek. I'd nicked him just a smidgen. On purpose, of course.

"You have to watch your back out here in the wild lands," I warned him. "There are monsters everywhere."

His eyes grew wide. I wiped his blood off on his shirt, then walked away.

"Showing off in front of vampires?" Harker commented as he joined me at the edge of the deck.

"They are easily impressed by flashy moves."

"And you managed to scratch him without seriously maiming him."

"Well, I do have skills, you know."

"You've improved." Harker looked thoughtful.

"Do I detect a hint of approval in your tone?"

"Perhaps just a hint." His eyes hardened as they panned across my body. "You've changed," he repeated. "But you still have a long way to go if you want to hold your own with the angels."

I leaned on the railing, lifting a brow at him. "Are you challenging me to a duel?"

"Are you accepting?"

"All right. When this is over. But I have to warn you, I fight dirty."

Harker laughed. "Indeed."

Nero came up behind us. "We're here. Time to go."

The supernaturals covered the lands beneath us. There were hundreds of them. The airship circled around them, flying over a small forest a few miles away. The plan was for us to drop down there and stealthily sneak up on the army.

Basanti pushed the vampires, witch, and elemental

toward the edge of the deck. "Come on, time to go." She spoke loudly, command ringing in her voice. It was the sort of voice used to train Legion soldiers.

"We're not descending," the Sea King observed.

"Of course not," she told him. "We can't land. The monsters feed on magic. They will tear the ship apart. It needs to stay up here."

"Then how will we get up to the ship again?" the Sea King asked, panic straining his voice.

Basanti showed off her watch. "I have a remote to summon the ship back to us when we're done."

The Vermillion vampire glanced at her watch, calculation gleaming in his eyes. "And any of us can activate it?"

"Any Legion soldier can."

"And what about the rest of us? What if we need to activate it?" the Snowfire vampire demanded.

"Ah, planning on taking off without us?" Constantine Wildman said.

"Of course not. But what if we don't all survive this? If we can't get back to the airship, we'll be stranded here."

Basanti grinned at the vampire. "You really believe that you will survive when four soldiers of the Legion do not?"

The Snowfire vampire shut his mouth.

"Enough talk," Nero said, his voice crisp. Like a whip. "Jump."

Constantine Wildman looked over the edge of the airship. "We're several hundred feet up in the air."

"Then you'd better all hold onto your buddy." Basanti grabbed the witch and swung him onto her back.

Harker took the Sea King. Nero carried the Vermillion vampire. And I got the Snowfire vampire who'd admired my hair. Lucky me.

"You can't fly," my passenger pointed out.

"No, but I excel at falling."

Then I jumped. The two angels dove over the edge of the airship, their dark wings extended. Basanti and I didn't have the luxury of feathers. We fell, using our elemental air magic to ride the wind currents down toward the ground. Basanti moved so gracefully, like a swan dancing on the wind. Or a surfer riding a wave.

I was…well, less graceful. With the help of my magic, I followed the air currents, but it was a bumpy ride. It was a vast improvement over the last time I'd fallen out of an airship, however.

"Are you sure you know what you're doing?" the Snowfire vampire asked me.

"Yes."

I felt the air currents rippling against my skin, hard and ragged. The vampire gripped me tightly.

"We're experiencing turbulence." His voice shook.

"That's nothing. The last time I fell out of an airship, it was so much worse. There aren't even any monsters trying to eat us this time."

He buried his head in my hair.

I threw an annoyed look over my shoulder. "Did you just smell my hair?"

"It's so pretty," he cooed. "It soothes my nerves."

"If you bite me, Fangs, I'll give you an express ticket all the way down to the ground."

I concentrated on slowing my fall, on making it smoother. I passed into a calmer patch of air. The wind was gentle, soft, caressing. Like silk ribbons tickling my skin.

We hit the ground a bit harder than I'd expected, but at least I stayed on my feet. We were even the first ones down. Obviously. We hadn't coasted so much as dropped.

The angels followed, landing smoothly. Nero set down

like a black swan on a serene lake. Harker's landing was nearly as smooth, but from the look of intense concentration on his face, I could tell he was still getting used to his wings. Basanti set down last. She moved almost like she had wings herself. Her magic was that easy, that smooth.

She grinned at me. "It's not a race, Pandora. There are no points for being first."

I returned the grin. "You're only saying that because you lost."

She laughed.

The Sea King slid off Harker's back. He staggered to the side and threw up.

"Oh, look. The Sea King is seasick," taunted the Vermillion vampire.

The Sea King straightened, wiping his mouth. "That's airsick, you moron."

"You are all pathetic," Constantine Wildman declared. "What will you do when we're surrounded by a horde of mindless, super-charged supernaturals?"

"We have the Legion here to protect us," the Sea King said.

The Vermillion vampire looked me up and down. He was clearly unimpressed. "You're putting your faith in the wrong hands. They ran scared from just two of these infected supernaturals. They are no match for a whole army of them."

I gritted my teeth. "We had to save a witch's life, to get her to safety."

The Vermillion vampire shot me a patronizing look. "Of course, dear girl."

I could tell he thought I was a coward, but I didn't have time to dwell on that right now. Plus I'd just remembered that I didn't give a shit what he thought.

We pressed on across the Black Plains, following the river

of supernaturals. They didn't seem to notice us at all. As we walked, I heard a voice in my head. It tugged at my mind, whispering commands, telling me to go to it.

"Do you hear that voice?" I asked the others.

Harker nodded. "Whoever is commanding this army is telepathic."

"Do you recognize the voice?" I asked him.

"No. But it sounds so…"

"Godly," I supplied.

He frowned. "Yes."

So was a god actually behind this?

The Snowfire vampire spun around, magic sizzling across his skin, building up.

"He's succumbing!" I shouted.

Basanti shot him in the chest.

I looked down at the vampire's unmoving body. Man, she'd moved fast. She'd managed to get him before he'd powered up, before he'd grown too strong to take down just like that.

"He's not dead," I noticed.

"No. It's a heavy sedative, something from Nerissa," she replied. "It will only last a few hours."

"What if it takes longer than that to stop this?"

"If it takes longer than that, we're likely already dead anyway," Harker told me.

"Since when did you get so dour?" I asked him.

"Becoming an angel is like a kick in the teeth, a splash of ice water, of reality," Nero said.

I looked at them, frowning. "Am I the only one who thinks we aren't marching to our deaths?"

The Sea King's body quaked. Basanti shot him too. "Yes."

"Is she kidding?" I asked Nero. "I can't really tell."

He gave her a long, hard look, then declared, "Neither can I."

"Basanti, you're getting stronger," Harker said. "Dare I hope that you've decided to join us in the dog race to the top?"

Basanti grinned at him. "I find myself suddenly motivated."

"Leila's influence?" he asked.

"That and my desire to kick your ass."

Chuckling, Harker set his hand on her shoulder, and Nero gripped her other shoulder. They were having fun. Genuine fun. The three of them had once been best friends. I could see a hint of that former bonding between them, of that camaraderie they'd lost. That alone almost made this catastrophe worth it.

We passed by infected supernaturals, none of whom paid us any notice. Their eyes were all turned upward, up to a raised platform. We'd made it to the core of the army, where their commander stood, staring down on them.

It was Stash. He was the voice I'd heard in my head. He was the one controlling the supernatural army.

22

THE WAR COMMANDER

I blinked my eyes a few times, but the illusion did not fade. Because it wasn't an illusion. This was all very real. Stash was controlling the infected supernaturals. He was behind this.

Of all the possibilities, that was one I would never have guessed. Stash was such a great guy. He wasn't a criminal mastermind or a war leader. The shifters had only sent him to the meeting because the pack leaders couldn't put aside their differences long enough to pick which of them would go. They'd sent the black sheep, the lone wolf, the one with no connection to any of them—so that no pack was slighted.

They sure as hell hadn't sent him because Stash held any position of power in their ranks. Nor did he want to. He tended bar, arm-wrestled for dollar bills, and did all other sorts of odd jobs. He seemed perfectly content doing that. And, most of all, he was my friend. I knew he was a good person.

"You'll often find that you don't know people at all," Nero told me. "Especially your friends." His gaze slid over to Harker.

"For the millionth time, Nero, I would never hurt Leda."

Nero glared at him in silence. Harker glared back. So much for camaraderie.

I stepped between them. "Stop. There's no time for this. "Are we sure Stash is the one controlling all those supernaturals? I just can't believe it."

"He is standing up there, overlooking them all like a war general," Harker pointed out.

It was hard to argue with what was right in front of my face. Stash stood up on that platform, tall and proud, with a confidence that showed he knew he was in charge. All that was missing was the battle helmet with a big crimson plume.

I looked across the army. The way they looked at Stash made everything all too clear. They saw him as their leader. Spelled, compelled, powered up—they wouldn't hesitate to die for him.

There were hundreds of supernaturals around us. They had all changed. They bore little resemblance to the people they'd once been. I could no longer tell the difference between vampires or witches, elementals or shifters. They were all one now, all the same. They weren't individuals; they were a horde. And with their uncommon magical might, they were a force to be reckoned with. I had a sinking suspicion that the naysayers in my group might be right. There was a pretty good chance we wouldn't walk away from this.

Stash's supernatural soldiers lifted their voices and sang. It was a low sound that started in one corner then spread to the whole army, growing louder with every verse. They were all singing in unison, like they were linked. Like they were one.

It was a beautiful, terrible song that resonated deep inside of me. It was a war song, I realized. I didn't understand the words, but something about it felt familiar, like I'd heard it before. It sounded old, ancient even. It was a song as old as time itself.

The melody sang to me, humming through my body, uplifting me. I felt my blood pumping faster through my veins, my magic soaring, my adrenaline raging. I felt so powerful, like I could take on a god. I bottled the euphoria. I might be immune to Angel Fever, but this song was speaking to my soul. I couldn't allow myself to get caught up in it. I had to stay focused.

"Appearances can be deceiving," I told the others. "Yes, Stash is standing up there. But how can he control all those supernaturals anyway? He is a shifter, not a siren. And not a telepath. He doesn't have this kind of magic. He couldn't have created Angel Fever."

Nero stared across the field where Stash stood on the platform, directing his army. "Look at his eyes."

Stash's eyes were shimmering oddly, like they weren't reflecting the sun's natural light. There was some other light —some other magic—inside of him.

"He's infected too," Nero said. "I can see it in his eyes. Someone or something is speaking through him."

"Possession?" I wondered. "His powers come from light magic. Can a god possess someone?"

"Yes, in the same way a demon can, a god can speak through someone." Nero was watching Harker. "But it's not a god speaking through him. Whatever this is, it's something else entirely. The infection changed him differently than the others."

"Why?"

"Perhaps it was by chance," said Nero. "Or perhaps it was intentional. What does every army need?"

"Someone to command it."

Nero nodded.

"Stash is that war commander," I said.

Constantine Wildman's body shook. His face crinkled up, like he was trying to fight the infection. Basanti pointed her gun at him.

"My mind is not gone yet, Captain Somerset." Constantine Wildman dug his fingers inside his pocket, pulling out the vial Nerissa had given him.

He drank down the potion to slow the effects of Angel Fever. Nerissa had dubbed it Demon Juice. Harker hadn't found that name any more amusing than Angel Fever.

The witch's body stopped shaking. He sucked in a few deep breaths, then tucked the empty vial into his coat pocket.

He pulled out a gun. "I'm not going to lose my mind."

Almost as soon as he said it, the tremors returned. The fever wasn't giving up. His hands shook so hard that he nearly dropped his gun. Sweat poured down his face. He was fighting the change. And it was fighting back. Hard.

"The effects are stronger here, at the core of the army, surrounded by the infected on all sides," Nero observed. "Nerissa's juice doesn't work as well here."

"It worked well enough." Constantine Wildman steadied his hands and pointed the gun at Stash.

"That won't work," Basanti told him. "All the infected have been too resilient."

"The bullets are spelled. It will work if I shoot him in the head."

"Maybe we should shoot *you* in the head," the Vermillion vampire said. "You don't look like you have long before you lose your mind and go all primitive on us."

"I am fine. But soon none of us will be fine, this whole

world won't be fine, not if we don't stop that shifter." The witch moved his gun to follow Stash's movements. "I have a clear shot. A bullet to the head, and this will all be over."

Harker exchanged glances with Nero. "It didn't work last time, but we could give it a shot."

"No. We are most certainly not giving it a shot," I growled. "I can't believe we are even discussing this. That's my friend!"

"He is controlling the whole army," the witch said. "If we kill him, we end this."

"No, he is infected too, just like the rest of them. He isn't behind this."

"He is the source of this. He is the reason they are infected."

"How do you figure that?" Harker asked him.

"Because he can control them. That is not insignificant. The infection must have started with him."

He said it like it made perfect sense. Except it didn't. Not at all.

"That doesn't make any sense," I told him.

He gave his hand a dismissive wave. "Of course it does."

I narrowed my eyes at him. "What are you not telling us?"

"I told you what I know: that he is the source of this plague, and he must die to end it. You just stubbornly refuse to believe it."

"No." I bit out the word. "You aren't using your messed-up logic to justify killing an innocent man. This isn't a witch hunt. What if you kill him, and the others aren't cured? Are you just going to keep shooting people until there's no one left?"

"Do you have a better idea of how to end this?" he asked

me. "This is how the Legion works. Your hammer hits hard and far, and you pick up the pieces later."

"He has a point," Basanti told Nero.

Nero seemed thoughtful, like he was considering the idea of shooting Stash. No, there was nothing to consider!

"This is madness," I told them all. "You can't actually be thinking about shooting Stash. This isn't his fault. He's a victim, just like the rest of them. We don't murder victims. We protect them."

"Honey, you have a very idealistic view of what the Legion does and does not do," the Vermillion vampire said. "I hate to say this, but I'm with the witch on this one. The shifter is the key to this. It's us or him, and I have no intention of losing my mind. It's an easy choice."

"And this is where *you* don't understand the Legion. It's not a democracy, and you don't get a vote," I snapped at him.

"Perhaps I don't." The Vermillion vampire looked at Nero. "But he does. What say you, General Windstriker? Listen to your sweetheart and the infection spreads across the Earth like wildfire, consuming humanity? Or listen to reason, and it all ends here?"

Nero's expression was as hard as marble.

"Nero?" I asked.

But before he could speak, Stash let out a roar, a sonic punch of agony and relief. The magical release rippled through the crowd like a shockwave, hard and heavy. It felt like an enormous building had just dropped on top of us, crushing us into the ground.

The crowd fell to its knees. Basanti, Nero, Harker, and I stayed up. Constantine Wildman's hands hit the blackened ground. The Vermillion vampire fell down next to him.

Then Stash's army rose and turned as one, facing us down.

Stash had risen from the platform. He was now several feet off the ground, his wings spread wide. White and silver tipped with orange, they beat in a slow, powerful rhythm. Stash had become an angel.

23

DIVINE ORIGINS

*S*tash was an angel. Angel Fever had progressed beyond anything we'd seen before. The name had been meant as a joke, a stab at the Legion of Angels by some of New York's disgruntled supernaturals. I didn't think they'd really expected the magic infection to create a real angel. And that was exactly what Stash was now, feathers and all.

Beside me, Nero's expression was wary, like he was calculating how hard it would be to take out Stash now that he was an angel. Harker wore a similar expression. I could almost see the battle against Stash playing out in their eyes.

Basanti held a gun in each hand, watching Stash like he might explode at any second. She had one gun pointed at him. Her other gun was aimed at Constantine Wildman. The witch was on the ground near her feet, kneeling like all the other infected people.

"This isn't possible," Nero said. "For someone to become an angel, it requires divine magic. No spell could have done this."

"If he's really like an angel now, it's going to be a bitch to

207

take him down. We should have shot him when we had the chance," Harker said.

"How can you say that? He is a victim in this."

Stash flew up, several of his feathers twirling in the air, as though they were caught in an invisible cyclone. White, gold, and orange—they danced on the wind. His army watched his every move, transfixed.

When he spoke, his voice bellowed, shaking the very ground beneath my feet. "For centuries, we have been pawns in this war between heaven and hell, between gods and demons. The war they brought here. The war that savaged our lands, boiled our oceans, crumbled our cities. But today is the day we make a stand. Today is the day we take back our world and expel these outsiders, gods and demons both."

His army cheered.

Harker pointed at Stash. "You call that a victim? He's a threat, Pandora."

They aren't wrong, Leda, Stash spoke in my mind. From my friends' expressions, he was speaking to them too.

He landed in front of me. His glistening wings tucked in against his back.

"I am a threat," he said to me, speaking aloud this time. "The threat that will end the gods' injustice once and for all."

The crowd roared with approval.

Constantine Wildman rose to his feet with difficulty, his face strained. He was fighting back, resisting the magic taking over his mind and body. Nerissa's potion was helping him. Step-by-step, he moved toward Stash.

But it was not enough. Stash waved his hand, and just like that, the witch dropped back down to his knees. His eyes flickered about, as though caught in a trance. Elemental magic sizzled on his hair.

"The infection has settled in fast this time," I commented.

"I can turn any one of them in an instant now," Stash said. "I've gained powers you could only dream of, Leda."

"Listen to yourself, Stash. You are forcing people to do things against their will. That's exactly what you *don't* do, why you're not in a pack. You believe in choice. You are sick, Stash. This spell has messed with your mind. This isn't you."

He let out a pained laugh. "This *is* me, Leda. It always has been. I just didn't know it." His eyes were glowing, dilated. He looked at the witch and said, "Tell them."

When Constantine Wildman spoke, his voice was distant and dreamy. "Stash is the child of a shifter mother. Her name was Eveline. She was a Chicago werewolf pack leader. Leader of the strongest shifter pack in the city."

Shifter magic was inherited; you couldn't be made into one. Not like a vampire. Shifters were born, vampires were made.

"Eveline was scarred at an early age, so she wasn't considered a great beauty," Constantine Wildman continued. "But she was one of the best warriors in the world. Her skills were highly prized—and admired. She had no shortage of lovers. One of them was the angel Sirius Demonslayer."

The witch paused, as though for dramatic effect. That must have been Stash conducting his performance. "Another of her lovers was a god of heaven. And it was that god who fathered Stash."

I blinked at Stash. So that meant…it meant he was a demigod. Like Nyx.

I thought back, running through every time I'd seen Stash. I tried to find any hints that would have clued me into his divine origins. I couldn't think of a single thing.

"Twenty years ago, my mother fell in love with the god,"

Stash said. "But matings between gods and mortals are frowned upon. Gods guilty of such matings lose face with the other gods. When my father found out she was pregnant, he tried to kill her."

"That's horrible," I said. But it wasn't surprising.

"My mother barely escaped with her life. She made a deal with a witch coven who had recently grown very powerful. It was said they could perform miracles. They cast a spell on her. The next time my father came for her, he stabbed her in the belly, and she died. He thought he'd killed me too, but I lived, protected inside a magic shell in her womb."

"How did the witches have enough magic to fool a god?" I asked. I'd never heard of any witch possessing that kind of power.

"They didn't. They used my mother's life force to shield me. She faced my father knowing she wouldn't survive. When she died, the power of her magic, of her life, fueled the spell."

Just like the gods had expected Nero to use the magical release of our bond—of my death—to power the Magitech barrier in the City of Ashes.

"My aunt later recovered me from my mother's body and ran far away. The witches' spell didn't just cloak me from my father. It buried the magic I'd received from him, hiding what I really was. I had only my mother's shifter magic. People who knew her believed that Sirius Demonslayer was my father, and that the two of them—and me, their unborn child—had died in battle."

"And you never knew the truth?" I asked him.

"No. Angel Fever brought out the magic I'd received from my father. At first, I didn't realize what was happening. It took some time before my mind could focus. I didn't remember the flashes of my power returning, piece by piece.

It wasn't until all my powers returned that I realized what had happened to me. That's when I fled to the Black Plains."

"How did the contagion start?" I asked him. "Who did it? Who unleashed Angel Fever?"

"It was you and Nero Windstriker."

I blinked. "*We* did this?"

"Not intentionally," Stash said. "When you broke the seal in the City of Ashes, you released the sirens trapped inside the vault." He looked at Constantine Wildman. "It turns out the witches who made a pact with my mother had grown strong by stealing talismans and other immortal objects of power from a siren clan. The sirens came knocking at the witches' doorsteps, seeking revenge. They planned to expose the witches' trickery, including my escape from death. To keep their secret—and keep themselves safe from my father's ire—the witch coven trapped the sirens inside the vault in the City of Ashes. It took all the magic in their stolen immortal artifacts to do it."

"So when Nero and I broke the seal…"

"The sirens escaped their twenty-year prison."

I gestured toward the witch. "How is he involved in this? Do you know?"

"I can read every thought in his scheming head. When the sirens got free, they decided to plot their revenge on the witch coven who had betrayed them."

I found myself unsurprised that Constantine Wildman had stolen magic from the sirens. He really was a sleazeball.

"The sirens wanted to expose the witches' trickery of my father, knowing he would come down hard on them. So they traveled to New York and found Constantine Wildman. Disguising themselves, they met with him. They played on his greed to sell him a spell that would make his coven more powerful than any other witch coven on Earth, a spell that would give them powers to rival the Legion of Angels itself. The witches had grown tired of not being powerful warriors like the vampires and shifters. They took the bait."

"But they didn't get what they bargained for," I said.

"Oh, they did. The witches gained powerful magic. The sirens simply failed to tell them that their bodies couldn't handle this unnatural flux of magic. Everyone the spell touched would lose their mind."

"Those sirens sound very vengeful," I commented.

"They were locked up for two decades, Leda. Of course they are vengeful," he said. "But we don't have only the sirens to thank for this. The witches played their part as well. In their greed, they forgot one very important thing: making a deal with a siren never ends well. Sirens are master negotiators and every deal they make comes with two prices: the price you make in payment and the unexpected price that comes later.

"The sirens knew the spell the witches had used to hide my magic because it was one of their own, a spell cast using an amulet. If Constantine Wildman remembered the amulet twenty years later, the sirens compelled him, making him forget all about it. When one of his witches put it on, the seal holding my magic shattered. My angel magic slowly returned to me, one power at a time. But a piece of my magic broke off and went into the witch who had worn the amulet to perform the spell. The first time she used my magic, the song of the siren's spell infected her opponent's magic. It jumped from person to person, spreading across the supernatural population."

"They all have a piece of you in them. A piece of a demigod's magic," I realized. "That's why they have these powers."

"The sirens knew about my divine blood. And they knew

the spell would spread across the supernatural populations of the city. And then beyond. Angel Fever will soon cover the Earth."

"What do the sirens want?"

"To expose me. And, in doing so, to expose the witches to my father's wrath." Stash pounded his fist against the palm of his other hand. "But the gods won't be killing any of us," he promised. "The sirens' spell had unintended consequences, even for the sirens themselves," he said. "Because I am the reason they have their abilities—because a piece of my magic lies within them—I have power over anyone infected. I summoned them here for a purpose."

"To raise an army."

"Yes."

"Against their will."

"Yes," he said. "My true self has finally revealed itself." He indicated the army around him. "And so you see, Leda, I am a monster."

"No, you aren't," I argued "You are a good man."

His mouth dropped into a sad smile. "You always want to see the good in everyone."

"You *are* good, Stash. That werewolf last night was you, wasn't it? You saved us from the infected vampire."

"Yes."

"See? Even mad with magic and power, you still looked out for your friends."

"Stop trying to paint me as a saint, Leda. I have done horrible things. Killed innocent people. I put everyone here under my spell to grow my army, to challenge the gods. I am no better than the sirens. My soul is black. I want revenge every bit as much as they do."

"You weren't yourself. You still aren't."

"No, for the first time in my life, I am completely myself. And this is what I am: a monster."

"You're just having trouble controlling the sudden influx of magic," I said, setting my hand on his arm.

He stepped away from me. "That is an excuse psychopaths use. The gods' laws of magic are very clear. We are responsible for our own acts. Lack of control is not an excuse." He looked at Nero. "Tell her."

"He speaks the truth," Nero confirmed.

"So you see, the gods do not share your opinion of me. In their eyes, I caused this. And they will punish me. My father will want to punish me most of all, whoever he is." Stash clenched his fists. "You should all get out of here. There is a storm of fury boiling inside of me, and I don't think I can control what I'll do."

"Like take on the gods?" Basanti asked.

Stash smirked grimly. "You know a thing or two about that, don't you?"

I looked at him in confusion.

"You are blind. You are *all* blind." Stash's gaze shifted to Nero. "Even you. For next to the power of a god, even an archangel is nothing. Next to the power of a demigod, you are nothing."

Green and gold magic burst out of his hands. It slammed into Basanti, peeling back layers of illusion, dissolving them. She wasn't Basanti at all. The strands of the shifting spell melted away, revealing Nyx, the First Angel of the Legion.

24

SHIFTER'S SHADOW

I looked at Nyx, squinting my eyes. "Where is Basanti?"

"At Storm Castle. She never left."

The realization of what Nyx's words meant hit me. "It was you all this time?"

Her red lips spread into a smile. "Yes."

That explained why news of Storm Castle was so hush-hush right now. No people were allowed in or out without Nyx's permission. It wasn't just the usual secrecy that surrounded the rebuilding of a Legion stronghold. Nyx was protecting her deception, so no one on the outside knew Basanti was still there.

Nyx had been pretending to be her all this time, and I hadn't even guessed it. I'd thought my magic of Shifter's Shadow was strong, that I could see though magic illusions. I'd thought I knew what I was doing. I had gotten used to this so quickly, to depending on my magic, for things to come to me just like that. I'd taken it all for granted.

But I wasn't powerful, and I didn't know a thing—not

compared to the First Angel, a demigod. Compared to Nyx's magic and might, I was nothing.

I had to admit it was a pretty massive blow to my ego. I hadn't realized how much my early success at the Legion had all gone to my head. Well, there was nothing like an experience like this one to bring my feet back down to the ground.

Harker and Nero were staring at Nyx. From the looks on their faces, this revelation was a blow to their egos too. The two angels hadn't realized it was Nyx either.

"Why are you here?" I asked her.

Nyx chuckled. "Blunt as always, I see." Now that the illusion of her shifting spell had faded, her charisma had returned. And her magic. Her long, black hair swirled in the air around her, flowing like it was underwater. "I've been keeping an eye on my newest angel. And on my newest archangel."

Harker and Nero both did their best to not look offended—Harker for being watched, Nero for being watched while he watched Harker.

"And then this mess gets dumped onto our plates." She turned her eyes, eyes as blue as the deep ocean, on Stash. "Fascinating. It seems I am not unique after all."

She truly looked fascinated rather than annoyed. It was behavior so unlike an angel, but, then again, Nyx was in a class all her own.

"Are you going to kill Stash?" I asked her.

As First Angel of the Legion, it was her duty to uphold the gods' laws and keep the Earth safe. Stash's army was a challenge to both.

"Of course not," she said. "A demigod is too rare to waste."

That was Nyx: practical to the core.

"But we really must put an end to this revolution." She

waved her hand to indicate the supernatural army. "They are drawing far too much attention to your existence."

"The gods have been walking all over us for centuries," Stash countered. "The Earth is not their playground. It is our home. *Ours.*"

There was power in that word. It rippled through the air, shaking me from the inside.

"That's the influx of magic speaking," Nyx told him calmly, apparently unaffected by his power. Or maybe she was just really good at hiding it. "All of us with divine blood tend to get territorial. The gods are not to blame for what happened to you and to all these people. It was the sirens' revenge. And the witches' greed."

"The gods created the situation," he replied, his jaw clenched hard. "And one god is very much involved, the one who impregnated my mother, the one who killed her. That god is the reason I am here."

She gave her hand a dismissive wave. "It makes no sense to blame the reason you are alive. I will help you learn to control your power, Stash. And, when you've had a chance to see things more clearly, to find your father. But you really must put an end to this revolution. We must cure these people."

Stash's eyes panned across his army. "I can't. I can't cure them," he admitted. "I don't know how. I only just now learned to control them. If I could have controlled them all along, I would have stopped them from killing people." He shot me an apologetic look. "From killing those Legion soldiers."

"I know you would have stopped them," I told him. "You are a good person, like I said."

Stash gave me a half-smile. "The jury is still out on that, sweetness."

"I will help you cure them. We'll do it together." Nyx extended her hand to him.

Stash took it.

"Close your eyes," she said.

Stash looked at her, his face hard.

"You're going to have to trust someone. And believe it or not, I know what you're going through." Magic sparked in her eyes.

"How can you possibly know what I'm going through?" he demanded. "You were born an angel. You always knew who you were, what you were."

"That's not entirely true. For a time, I was lost."

"Lost?"

"It's a long story. A story for another time." Her tone was hard, leaving no room for argument. "Now close your eyes."

He obeyed.

"See the magic that connects you to them. You are at the center of a web of magic that starts with you, reaching out," she said, her voice dreamy, almost soothing. "When the spell locking your magic broke, something happened. Your magic —fragile, volatile from being bottled up for so long— exploded out of you. Pieces of it grafted onto them, changing them." She looked at Constantine Wildman, who was kneeling at her feet. "There is no spell that can give you the powers of other supernaturals," she told the witch. "Nothing but Nectar or Venom can do that. You all have these powers because a piece of Stash's magic is in you."

The witch blinked. His mind was clearly somewhere else.

Nyx walked behind Stash, setting her hands on his shoulders. "That piece of magic in them will eventually kill them because their bodies are rejecting it. They can't handle it. Though, admittedly, most of them will go mad long before that point. So, you see, your army will be dead before it can challenge anyone."

Stash swallowed hard, his face etched with guilt. "How do we help them?"

"You need to draw those pieces of your magic out of them, like shrapnel from a wound. Draw them out, absorbing them back into yourself. Then their minds and magic will be back to normal. And your magic will be whole once more. Feel those parts of you in them, draw them into you." She nodded. "Good. Nice and slow."

I didn't see anything. Fireworks weren't exploding overhead. I didn't even see any tiny magic sparkles pulsing. But I felt...something. Like thousands of invisible fireflies were flying around us—not seen but felt.

The infected supernaturals began dropping to the ground —dozens at a time, peppered throughout the crowd. After the last people fell, Stash sighed in relief, as though an enormous load had been lifted from him.

Nyx peeled her hands off his shoulders and circled back around to face him. "It is done. When they awake, they will be back to normal." Then, in a flash of movement, she grabbed Constantine Wildman by his crushed-velvet jacket and quickly slit his throat with a black dagger. "All but one." She tossed the dead witch's body to the ground.

The angels didn't blink. I didn't either. I was too busy gaping at Nyx in shock. I knew why the First Angel had done it. Constantine Wildman had created this problem by trying to gain magic his witches couldn't have, magic by forbidden means. Nyx's response was swift. Merciless. That was the gods' justice, the Legion's justice. Nyx might have her moments of humanity, but she was still the First Angel.

Stash didn't look at the witch's body. He was trying to distance himself, his emotions—to block them off so that they didn't get in the way. That was the angel in him shining through.

"Will any of them remember anything?" he asked her.

"When your magic broke off onto them, their conscious minds were clouded," she replied, sheathing her dagger. "I have wiped away what few memories they have of the experience. It is better this way. For them. And most especially for you."

I tried to fathom how much magic it required to wipe so many minds. Hundreds of minds at once. It was no wonder Nyx had been able to fool us all—even the angels—with her disguise. Every time I forgot what she was, something like this happened to beat the reminder into me. Nyx wasn't just an angel. She was a demigod.

And so was Stash, I reminded myself again. Now that his magic was unlocked, he was just like Nyx.

Nyx looked at me, amusement dancing in her eyes. "Well, not quite like me," she responded to my thoughts. "He still needs to learn to control his magic."

"And what of the infected people who are not here, those at the Legion?" I asked.

"They are back to normal as well."

I pulled out my phone and dialed.

"What are you doing?" Harker asked me.

"Calling Nerissa."

Nyx chuckled. It was the sound of purring kittens and magic rainbows—the kind with pots of gold waiting at the end. "By all means, don't take my word for it."

Nerissa answered the phone.

"What's the situation?" I asked her.

"Everyone infected just fell unconscious. What did you do?"

"We found a cure. When they wake up, they'll be fine."

She whistled across the phone line. "Your ability to perform miracles never ceases to amaze me."

"I can't take the credit this time. We have the First Angel to thank."

"The First Angel?"

"I'll tell you all about it later," I said. Then I hung up.

"You can't tell her everything," Nyx told me as I put my phone away. She pressed the button on her watch that summoned the airship.

"Why is that?" I asked her.

"We'll discuss that shortly." She looked up at airship hovering above us. "First, let's load up these sleeping beauties."

***

WITH FOUR ANGELS, THE LOADING OF THE AIRSHIP went fast. When the hundreds of sleeping supernaturals were on board, we took off. The airship dropped us off near to an abandoned building on the Black Plains. As it flew back to New York to deliver Nyx's 'sleeping beauties' to the Legion office, the First Angel motioned for Nero, Harker, Stash, and me to follow her into an old building.

We were standing inside that building now, waiting for her to tell us why she'd brought us here. It looked like an old farm house. The wooden walls were dark, decaying. The support beams were rotting from the water that gushed through the house. I wasn't sure if the builders had built this house on top of a waterfall, or if the waterfall had come later. I did know that the water was slowly but surely tearing the house apart.

"Why are we here?" I asked Nyx, my voice a little nasal. I had to hold my breath to not gag on the moldy stench.

"I needed a place deep inside the wild lands, away from spies."

"Whose spies?" I asked. "Gods or demons?"

Nyx smiled. "Yes."

She typed a message into her phone. A moment later, two men in black cloaks led five sirens into the room.

The sirens were beautiful. There were four women and one man—all with long silver hair, braided back from their faces. All with eyes that shone like sapphires and skin that shimmered like crushed diamonds. They looked exactly how I'd always imagined unicorns in human form to be.

The sirens wore headbands adorned with gems that matched their necklaces, bracelets, and ankle jewelry. Strings of gemstones were woven into their bright and colorful clothes too. And into the sandals on their feet.

Nyx waved to the cloaked men, a silent gesture to execute the beautiful sirens, to end this just as she had killed Constantine Wildman on the battlefield. The men in black moved quickly, their blades slashing like lightning. The sirens dropped all at once to the ground, dead.

"What are you doing?" Stash asked, horror shining in his eyes as they panned across the beautiful corpses on the ground.

"The same thing I did back on the battlefield: keeping your secret," she told him. "Besides the people in this room, the sirens were the last living souls who knew what you truly are."

"What will happen if someone finds out what I am?" he asked.

"One step at a time."

I looked closely at Nyx's two henchmen for the first time, the men the First Angel was trusting with Stash's secret. The two men looked unremarkable, plain. They had the sort of faces that blended into a crowd, that thousands of men just like them had. Each one was a stock model henchman, the kind you ordered out of a catalogue. Someone you weren't supposed to spare a second glance—or remember after the fact.

And yet there was something else about them. Something familiar. Nyx's revelation had reminded me that things weren't always as they appeared.

I squinted at them, trying to figure out who they really were. They weren't just henchman cookie cutouts. They were more than that.

Nyx looked from me to her two henchman, a smile curling her lips. "Very good, Pandora."

She nodded at the men in black. Their disguises melted away, revealing Ronan and Damiel.

ANGELS, GODS, AND DEMIGODS

*N*ero stared at his father in shock. "What are you doing here?"

"Did you really think I wouldn't notice the return of one of my angels? Especially one as colorful as Damiel." Nyx made a sound that was almost a giggle. "It's adorable that you think I'm so gullible, Nero."

"How long have you known?" he said with false calmness. Through our bond, I could feel his unrest.

"Since right after your glorious escapade in the Lost City," she said. "After I left Leda's house, Damiel came to me in secret with news of the sirens sleeping in the City of Ashes. He also told me rumors of another demigod, one whose true identity was hidden away by an immortal amulet that belonged to the sirens."

"Did you know it was Stash?" I asked Damiel.

"No. I had no idea who it was. For all I knew, it could have been you."

"Me?"

He shrugged, a gesture so casual for an angel. "A

demigod orphaned twenty years ago. It seemed to fit. And you have to admit that you are unusual."

Nyx's blue eyes met mine. "Indeed, she is."

"All I knew was the sirens trapped in the City of Ashes were the key," Damiel said.

"Damiel also brought me rumors of a god who wanted to see those sirens released, wanted to have the demigod exposed—and create controversy and strife for the other gods," said Nyx.

What a shocker. "Which god?" I asked.

"When you two broke the seal in the City of Ashes, you released the sirens," Ronan told me and Nero. "One of the gods wanted them released, wanted this whole thing to blow up. But until Nero's evaluation after the trials, we didn't know which god it was."

"It was Faris."

I turned in surprise at Harker's voice.

"Faris wanted the sirens released," he continued. "And sirens aren't the only thing that got loose. Much, much more was trapped in that vault. Including ghosts."

Ghosts. That was another name for telepaths, who were so highly valued for their magic that the gods hunted them all down and 'invited' them to come work for them.

Nero had once told me that unlike every other supernatural on Earth, telepaths' powers weren't born from the gods' magic. They'd been here first, before the gods and demons had come to the Earth. And because of that, they possessed some telepathic abilities that were even beyond the gods' powers. In fact, the ghosts were why the gods and demons had come to Earth in the first place. The armies of light and dark magic had fought over telepaths on many other worlds —so much so that there were hardly any ghosts left.

"How do you know telepaths were trapped in that vault in the City of Ashes?" I asked Harker.

"After you returned, Faris gave me a heads-up to look for escaped ghosts, to capture them for him," he said.

Nyx gave Harker an approving nod.

"Interesting," Ronan commented. He looked upon Harker with surprise, which wasn't an expression you often saw on a god's face. "Nyx knows you well. She said you were an honorable man. Misguided, but honorable. She was sure that when confronted with everything, all the trouble one god went through to swing a punch at another, that you would turn on him."

Nyx smirked at Ronan. "He is Leila's protege, after all."

The God of War sighed like he'd just lost a bet.

I turned to Harker. "Faris is the god you serve. The God of Heaven's Army."

"Yes," Harker said, his jaw tight.

"Faris has been collecting telepaths since the gods' arrival on Earth. That is no secret," said Nyx.

"What was a secret was his brother's indiscretions," Ronan added.

"Zarion?" I gasped. "The God of Faith and patron of the Pilgrims? His high and holiness himself slept with a mortal?"

"Apparently," Nyx said. She didn't look the least bit surprised. She knew the gods a lot better than I did. "And Faris, ever looking for ways to take a stab at his brother, wanted to expose him, to embarrass him in front of the other gods on the council."

"This was set up by Faris to expose Stash," I realized. "Everything, including Nero's trials. Faris knew we would break the seal to power the barrier—and that it would release the sirens, who'd been trapped and plotting their revenge for twenty years."

"Yes," said Ronan. "Faris knew the sirens would find a way to expose Stash, which would in turn expose his brother's indiscretions. The two of them have been fighting for centuries. It was only a matter of time before one of them found something he could use against the other."

"But why? They're brothers. Why would they want to hurt each other this badly?" I just couldn't get my head around that. I'd do anything for my brother and sisters. It didn't matter that we weren't related by blood. I loved them with all my heart.

"It is the way of gods and demons, pulling strings, playing with mortals," Ronan told me. "We've been doing it for millennia on many worlds."

I mulled that over, then said, "You are a god."

"Yes." His dark eyes twinkled with magic. He looked amused. The expression reminded me of Nyx.

"And yet you want to help us?" I asked.

"Nyx is very persuasive. And I once made the mistake of choosing the other gods over her, one I came to regret for centuries." Ronan reached out and took Nyx's hand. "I won't make that mistake again."

"How romantic," I teased them.

Nero shot me a disapproving look. Apparently I shouldn't tease demigods or their godly lovers.

Except I wasn't joking. I was dead serious. Ronan's words *were* very romantic. Especially for someone who was a soldier —and a god.

Nyx just chuckled. "Don't let Ronan fool you. This is as much business as pleasure. There's a divide amongst the gods. Factions are forming in heaven. The demons know it. That's why they've been testing the waters so much lately, trying to get a foothold on Earth. They are just waiting for the gods' council to stumble."

"How many divisions?" Nero asked.

"Too many," said Ronan. "Gods are not good at group acts. We prefer a solo performance, to be the main attraction. Alliances form, but at the end of the day, it will be every god for himself. Or herself."

"We cannot allow this to happen," Nyx insisted. "The gods must stick together. We must all stick together. Divided we are weak. Divided we fall."

"What about him?" Damiel looked at Harker. "You trust him, Faris's lackey?"

"I wouldn't have agreed to make him an angel if I didn't think he could be swayed. Leila always did say he's loyal. He just sometimes needs a kick to the head to realize which way was right." Nyx winked at Harker. "That's a direct quote, by the way."

"Leila is too soft, but she is an excellent judge of character," Damiel allowed. "She can see right through people."

"Cadence is the same way," said Nyx. "She always saw something in you, Damiel, past the darkness and scathing sarcasm. She loves you."

Damiel kept his expression guarded. Thinking about Cadence must have hurt. "All verbal flourishes aside, Nyx, you cannot deny what Harker has done."

"You have done far worse," she reminded him. "And it didn't take Harker two hundred years to come around."

"I'm not coming around. I'm simply choosing the lesser of two evils. Faris is a menace. Left to his rule, we will all burn—mortals and immortals alike."

"Plus he's trying to manipulate your son's beloved Pandora into exposing her brother." Nyx's smile was as ruthless as it was kind. She sure was an interesting contradiction. "Getting sentimental in your old age, old man?"

"Are you?" he retorted.

Nyx laughed, even as Nero glared at his father.

"Don't look at me like that, boy," Damiel said, his voice as hard as granite. "She already knew about Leda and her brother. She knows everything." His expression softened as he turned to wink at me.

I wondered if Nyx did indeed know *everything*. Did she know about the Guardians? She had spoken of Cadence in the present tense, as though she knew Nero's mother was still alive.

I decided not to share my thoughts. Instead, I bottled them up, hiding them behind my growing mental wall. That's what the angels and gods would have done—not shared their secrets unless they had to. I really was starting to think like them more and more.

"I did not realize Faris was acting against the other gods," Harker said. "But this recent situation has been…"

"Eye-opening?" I supplied.

"Yes," he agreed. "Eye-opening. It has made me realize Faris has his own agenda. When I joined the Legion, I swore to serve all the gods, not one single god. And I vowed to protect humanity. Faris is acting against that, against everything the Legion stands for. Against everything that I stand for. I wanted to end suffering, but my actions have instead caused so much of it."

"Good speech," Damiel said when Harker was finished. "How long did you practice it?"

I frowned at Nero's father. "How did you get to be so skeptical?"

"I was the leader of the Legion's Interrogators for many years, honey. I was paid handsomely to be skeptical."

"I know he is genuine." Stash spoke up. He set his hand on Harker's shoulder. "He regrets all that happened— and the part that he played in it." His gaze shifted to me.

"Especially how he hurt you, Leda. He wants to make it right."

"How do you know this?" Nero asked him.

"Because I can see into his soul," Stash said, as though that were the most normal thing in the world.

Nyx folded her arms across her chest, her black leather suit a soft whisper of movement. "Interesting."

"Interesting?" I asked.

"Every archangel and god has a few unique powers," she explained. "Looking into someone's soul, seeing who they truly are past the armor and magic, appears to be one of Stash's." She looked at Nero. "And you, General Windstriker? You've been watching Harker. What do you think? Can he be trusted?"

Nero met Harker's eyes for a moment. He looked at me, then back at Nyx. "I agree with Stash's assessment."

"Well, then. It's all settled." Ronan extended his hand to Harker. "Welcome to the right side. Screw up, and I'll kill you myself."

Harker did not look surprised by Ronan's bluntness. He met the god's eyes and shook his hand.

"Splendid," Ronan said. "Now here's what I need you to do."

26

TRAINING WITH ANGELS

I crossed the line on the running track, which marked the end of my forty-seventh mile this morning. But Harker, who was running in front of me, didn't slow down. He kept going. Nero was close on my tail, making sure I didn't slow down either. Man, it was a good thing we weren't human because my heart might have already given out. As it was, it just felt like it was going to burst through my chest. The two angels didn't believe in doing anything half-assed.

It had been several months since we'd faced Stash on the Black Plains. Nero hadn't completely forgiven Harker, but things were slowly getting back to the way they'd once been, back when they'd used to be friends.

"I can feel your eyes burning a hole through the back of my head, Nero," Harker said.

"Gods, I hope that's an exaggeration," I said. I was running between the two of them. Any laser stare would cut through me first.

"If you don't feel comfortable with me behind you, we could switch places," Nero told Harker.

ELLA SUMMERS

"So you can accuse me of staring at Leda's ass? I think I'll dodge that bullet."

I chuckled.

"Leda," Nero warned.

Uh-oh. I knew that tone.

Harker supplied Nero's words, the words I knew were coming. "If you can laugh, you're not running fast enough."

I was the reason for the rift between them, so it was only fitting that I was the reason for the mending of their friendship. They were united in their commitment to level up my magic by thoroughly kicking my ass.

Nero gave me a little psychic nudge in the butt, pushing me to move faster.

"How long have you been waiting to do that?" I demanded. If I hadn't been worried about tripping over my own feet at this speed, I'd have shot him an irked look over my shoulder.

"Ever since I first saw you in that running suit this morning," he told me.

"You can proposition her later, Nero. The First Angel wants Leda ready by the time the Crystal Falls Training comes around."

Harker was still leading the New York office, and he was still officially in charge of my training. Ronan had turned him into a double agent. He had to report back to Ronan on everything Faris told him.

"She'll be ready for the Crystal Falls Training," Nero said.

Nero was now Nyx's second in command. I called him the Second Angel, but he didn't seem to appreciate the title. I couldn't imagine why.

The Legion's New York office was his main home, but he wasn't here as often as I would have liked. He was meeting with Nyx all the time and going on lots of trips all over the world. He visited the Legion's offices in Nyx's stead to make sure things were running smoothly—and to assess the angels' loyalty to her. He also put out supernatural fires from time to time. And for those missions, he could select soldiers from any Legion office.

"She can't go to the training until she's gained psychic magic," Harker pointed out. "It's levels six and seven only."

"She'll be ready," Nero repeated.

"We'll need to increase her training sessions to up her psychic resistance."

Harker—and Nero when he was around—had been training my psychic resistance by blasting me with telekinetic spells. I'd ended each and every session with broken bones—and I hadn't felt any more resistant than I had on day one. There was always the chance that I'd survive my next dose of Nectar anyway, but I didn't like playing the lottery. And neither did the two angels training me.

"Maybe we need to try a different approach," I said.

"Like what?" Harker asked.

"I'm not sure."

"Less talking. More running," Nero told me. "If you get stronger, your magic will get stronger too. You just need a little push."

And with that said, he pushed me again with his psychic magic. I stumbled forward but recovered my stride. This wasn't the first time he'd done that, and it wouldn't be the last. I had two choices: I could either get more resistant to psychic attacks and not let his magic throw me off balance, or I could get faster so he couldn't psychic-punch me. As far as Nero was concerned, either case was a win. In either case, I got stronger. He was practical like that. I wondered if he realized how much like his father he truly was.

Damiel was now Nyx's advisor and private Interrogator.

He questioned people she didn't want anyone to find out about. He seemed happy to get out of the 'gilded cage' Nero had put him in.

Stash sometimes worked with Damiel and Nero on their missions. He was keeping his true identity a secret. It was safer for him. As long as the truth stayed buried, Faris couldn't use him to play war with his brother Zarion. Nyx and Ronan were training Stash in secret, growing his demigod powers. As Nero gave me another psychic nudge, I wondered if they were torturing Stash as much as Nero and Harker were torturing me.

Finally, we completed our final lap. Nero glanced at the time on his watch. "Nearly a minute faster than the last time we all ran together."

We hadn't all run together in over a week, not since Nero had left for his last mission. I'd been training alone with Harker. He wasn't easy on me either, but at least he didn't blast me with psychic energy when I was running. Or when I was lifting weights. I rubbed my head, remembering the loaded barbell I'd dropped on myself thanks to Nero.

"A minute faster." I grinned at them. "Pretty good, don't you think?"

Harker shot me a blank look, clearly unimpressed. "You need to shave another five minutes off that time."

Oh, great. Now there were two of them. All those people who fantasized about spending time alone with two angels didn't know what it really meant: pain. And more pain. If they'd known the truth, they wouldn't have made all those crude jokes to me.

I tossed Nero and Harker each a water bottle. Even angels needed to stay hydrated. I made a conscious effort not to aim the bottles at their heads. They were trying to help me. I had to remember that, even when it felt like they were trying to kill me.

I put on a big smile. "I'll get there. Don't worry. With you two by my side, how could I possibly fail?"

Harker took a long drink from his bottle, then said to Nero, "Haven't you warned her about tempting fate?"

"Leda doesn't believe in fate."

"That's right. I don't. I believe we all have the power to make our own way and to choose our own destiny." I set my hand on his arm and gave it a squeeze. "The power to do the right thing."

"Everyone can be saved?" He looked highly skeptical.

"Yes."

"What about Colonel Fireswift?" Harker asked.

I winced. "Ok, *almost* anyone."

Nero snorted.

"I guess I should amend that to: anyone who wants to be saved can be saved," I said. "Colonel Fireswift included."

"Funny you should say that."

I grimaced. "I don't think I like where that sentence is headed, Harker."

He draped a towel over his shoulders. "Because he's coming to New York next week."

"Do either of you have a mission that will take me out of New York next week?" I asked the two angels.

One of Harker's brows arched upward at me. "What happened to redeeming Colonel Fireswift?"

"I'm going to concentrate on saving the younger Fireswift first."

"Jace Fireswift. He's good." Harker looked at Nero. "Almost as good as you were. And he's determined. He also has a thing for your girl."

"That's not true," I told him. "Jace is my friend."

Harker laughed. Nero's eyes narrowed.

"His father had him go on a string of difficult missions during the past few months. Captain Fireswift has already gained psychic magic." Harker shot me a meaningful look. "You're falling behind your 'friend', Leda. He has the benefit of his natural magic and the fact that he's been training since he was a baby. If you don't get your act together, he'll beat you to the prize."

"What prize?"

"He'll be the first of you two to become an angel."

I rolled my eyes. "It's not a competition."

"Tell that to Jace Fireswift," replied Harker. "He's determined to become an angel before you."

"That's his father's influence, pressuring him."

"That might be part of it." A devilish gleam shone in his eyes. "But I'm sure he's also heard that you have a thing for angels."

Nero's water bottle burst inside his fist.

"Don't listen to Harker," I told him. "He's just trying to mess with you."

"I know. But that doesn't mean what he says isn't true."

I shook my head at Harker. "You are smarter than this. Nero is going to kick your ass if you keep annoying him."

Harker laughed. Nero glared at him, his face cold. Then, suddenly, he laughed too. I couldn't hold back my smile. It was nice to see them like this again. Friends again.

Nero tossed the crushed water bottle into the trash. "I have some things to attend to in my office." He set his hands on my cheeks, then leaned down and kissed me.

It was a quick kiss, but I had to admit it left me breathless nonetheless. And that wasn't just from the fifty miles we'd just run.

After Nero left the gym, I looked up at the clock. "Basanti is arriving soon from Storm Castle. Let's go greet her."

Harker nodded in agreement, then we headed down to the garage. We found her there, arguing with a mechanic who was accusing her of ruining the truck she'd checked out.

"I got attacked by a herd of savage bison," Basanti snapped. Her hair was coming out of her bun, and her face was smudged with dirt and oil. The truck parked behind her was splattered with blood. "Of course it's damaged. But once you rub off the blood, it won't look half as bad."

The mechanic shot her a look of absolute horror.

She threw up her hands in frustration. "Well, then just paint over it again. It's what you guys do anytime the slightest mark gets on any of our trucks." She turned her back on him and grinned at me and Harker. "I'm gone for a few months, and everyone gets promoted."

As the mechanic fussed over the truck's unwanted bloody paint job, I swooped in and gave her a hug. "I'm glad you're back."

Harker kissed her on the cheek, then we left the garage.

"Hiya," Alec greeted Basanti in the halls. "We've missed you. You get lost on the Black Plains?"

Basanti shot him a confused look, but he was already walking toward the gym, trailed by a group of initiates. Alec sometimes taught them how to shoot.

"Ok, why does everyone here think I've been on the Black Plains?" Basanti asked us later, after several other people in the halls had made similar comments to her. "I've spent the last few months at Storm Castle, helping with the repairs."

"Talk to Nero," I told her.

"How mysterious," Basanti said drily, glancing at my

back. "I don't see any wings on you, Leda, but you're talking more like an angel every day."

"I'll go with you," Harker told her, and the two of them walked toward Nero's office.

I headed for the stairwell. Jace met me on his way down.

"Hey," I said. "How were your missions?"

"My father sent me to the Wicked Wilds, the Forsaken Forest, and the Forgotten Desert."

"I heard you did some pretty impressive things." I pointed at the symbol of a psychic hand pinned onto his jacket below the words 'Captain Fireswift'.

"Yes." His gaze dipped to the shifter symbol on my sweatshirt. "I see you were promoted too."

"Yes, but not twice like you were."

His smile was satisfied. And the way he was looking at me was…strange. Like he wanted to impress me. Was Harker right?

No, I decided. Harker was just messing with me, making me imagine things. Jace Fireswift did *not* have a thing for me.

I told Jace what had happened while he was gone, minus the part where Stash turned out to be a demigod and where we'd met with Nyx, Damiel, and Ronan.

My tale must have been thrilling enough anyway because he sighed. "One of these days, I'm going to have a better story than you, Leda."

I smirked at him. "Bring it on."

After we parted ways, I went to my temporary shoebox of a room to change. After my apartment had exploded, I hadn't bothered to look for a new one. I had, however, encouraged Ivy and Drake to get one without me.

I stared at my bare room, which was hardly large enough for the bed and closet. A few of my clothes had miraculously survived Ivy blowing up our old apartment.

They hung in the closet, along with a whole lot of Legion leather.

"Leda."

I jumped in surprise at the sound of Nero's voice. I turned around to face him. His body filled up the doorway, making it look so small. And he didn't even have his wings out right now. He sure knew how to make an entrance. And, you know, just stand there.

"You have really got to stop doing that," I told him.

He closed the door behind him. My room got even smaller.

"Did you talk to Basanti?" I asked as I changed my clothes.

"Yes."

"And how did she take it?"

"That the First Angel spent days impersonating her? Surprisingly well. She wasn't even surprised. Being reunited with Leila has had an effect on her."

"It reminded her of the games you angels like to play?"

"She always knew about the games that angels play. She is just more accepting of them now."

I slipped into my jacket. "So, to what do I owe the pleasure of this visit, General?"

"I have something for you." He held out a small wrapped present.

"My birthday is next month."

"I am well aware of your birthdate, Leda."

Of course he was. He'd read it on my Legion application. He'd probably read everything on that sheet so many times, trying to figure me out. To decipher why I was really there. I sure hadn't written 'to find my brother, a telepath, and keep him out of the Legion's hands'. That wouldn't have gone over well.

I fingered the present's shiny wrapping paper. "It's very pretty. It even has a bow. Did you wrap it yourself?" I grinned at him.

"Just open the box, Pandora."

I chuckled. "Now *that* is a sentence I never thought I'd hear."

I tore off the beautiful wrapping paper and found a small jewelry box inside. The box was gold set with gemstones. It must have cost a fortune. What could possibly be inside? I lifted the lid to find a silver key, cushioned inside a bed of velvet.

"The keys to the kingdom?" I asked. I just couldn't help myself.

"The keys to your new apartment. *Our* new apartment." He watched me closely for my reaction.

I just blinked like an idiot.

"You didn't think I'd forgotten," he said.

He meant way back before the Gods' Trials, when I'd thought about how I wanted to live with him. I hadn't even said it aloud. I'd just thought it. He'd heard me—and remembered.

Why couldn't I stop blinking at him? Did I think he would disappear, that this would turn out to be nothing more than a dream?

"You've changed your mind." His voice was guarded, cautious.

"Are you kidding?" I kissed him. "Of course I haven't changed my mind. I would love to live with you."

"Good." The satisfaction rolled off his tongue.

"Good?"

"Exactly."

I snorted. "Sometimes you're so weird, Nero."

"I find that a peculiar statement coming from you."

"Oh, it's a compliment," I told him. "One hundred percent."

"If you would just pack up your things—"

I hastily tossed the meager contents of my closet into a box. It took about two seconds. "Ready."

His brows lifted, obviously impressed by my magic trick. "Then we can go see the apartment," he finished. "After which we'll have dinner and get in another training session."

"Hey, I have a different idea. Let's be crazy for a change and spice up the routine."

"What do you suggest?" I could almost see his mind working, shuffling through possible training programs.

I draped my arms over his shoulders. "Let's just lie on the sofa in our new apartment, watching TV while stuffing ourselves full of caramel popcorn until we enter a sugar-induced coma and fall asleep in each other's arms."

He stared at me for a moment, so long that I started to get worried I'd offended him. Then he brushed my hair behind my ear with a smile and declared, "That sounds perfect."

AUTHOR'S NOTE

If you want to be notified when I have a new release, head on over to my website to sign up for my mailing list at http://www.ellasummers.com/newsletter. Your e-mail address will never be shared, and you can unsubscribe at any time.

If you enjoyed *Shifter's Shadow*, I'd really appreciate if you could spread the word. One of the best ways of doing that is by leaving a review wherever you purchased this book. Thank you for your invaluable support!

The sixth book of *Legion of Angels* will be coming soon.

ABOUT THE AUTHOR

Ella Summers has been writing stories for as long as she could read; she's been coming up with tall tales even longer than that. One of her early year masterpieces was a story about a pigtailed princess and her dragon sidekick. Nowadays, she still writes fantasy. She likes books with lots of action, adventure, and romance. When she is not busy writing or spending time with her two young children, she makes the world safe by fighting robots.

Ella is the international bestselling author of the paranormal and fantasy series *Legion of Angels*, *Dragon Born*, and *Sorcery and Science*.

www.ellasummers.com